Caleb Anderson

Berkley's Bastards Book 1

KATHI S. BARTON

World Castle Publishing, LLC
Pensacola, Florida
Copyright © Kathi S. Barton 2021
Paperback ISBN: 9781955086639
eBook ISBN: 9781955086646
First Edition World Castle Publishing, LLC, July 26, 2021
http://www.worldcastlepublishing.com

Licensing Notes

Cover: Karen Fuller
Editor: Maxine Bringenberg

Chapter 1

Caleb let the tears fall down his cheeks. His mother, his hero, had taken her last breath, and he was having a hard time dealing with the pain of her leaving him. He knew she was no longer suffering. The drugs and things they'd been giving her since she took to her bed three weeks ago had taken care of that. But she had been there for him all his life, and he wasn't sure what he was going to do without her around.

"Sir, Hospice is here. They wish to come in and see her." He nodded and kissed his mother's cold hand before putting it under the blanket, which was over her body. "She'll be sorely missed, sir. Your mother was a great woman. One of a kind, if you were to ask me."

"I know you loved her too, Ben. She loved

everyone so much."

Nodding, the two men embraced for a few moments. Then he straightened up and moved out of the way for the people from Hospice to do what they needed.

Caleb found himself in the kitchen then. The cup of tea was just what he'd needed. Mary, Ben's wife, asked if his mother had passed. Nodding, a fresh stream of tears fell down his face, and she hugged him as well. He clung to the woman who had become his second mother in all these years and cried softly into her warm bosom.

"She'll be wondering what all the fuss is about if she were to look down on us now." He laughed a little. "That's my boy. You'll be simply fine, Caleb. It's why she left when she did. A real lady doesn't stay too long when there are other things to be taken care of. You'll be good because she raised you well."

"Mom and I couldn't have done it without you and Ben around all the time. I think when she had to work, she didn't mind leaving me here because the two of you were around." Mary nodded and said she'd do it all over again if asked. "I know you would. She knew too that leaving me now would be all right because of the two of you. You are staying on, right? You won't leave me here all alone?"

"What a thing to ask of me. Of course, we'll be here for you. When you find yourself a pretty little wife to come here, we'll be there for your children as well. However, I will tell you that if you decide to sell and move to another place, Caleb, we will go out west. I don't think I could get used to another home this late in my life. You know that." He did but didn't know about the pretty little wife. "You'll see. As soon as you're out and about again, women will be relieved to know you're back to work and such. Your momma, she told you not to mourn her too long, didn't she?"

"She said I was to dump her out of the bed and have the room redecorated as soon as her body was cold." He laughed and cried a little at that. "Mom was full of it all the way to the end. I'll miss her so much."

Crying again, he felt hands patting him on the back. Not just Mary's, but her husband's comforting hand as well. Letting himself grieve for a little bit, he sat up in the chair when Mary gave him a plate of little food, as she called it.

It was apple slices and peanut butter. Cheese and crackers with a bit of mustard on the side. Also, since he'd gotten older, she would put either a glass of wine with his little meal or a bottle of beer, neither of which he had the stomach for right now.

The nurse that had been with his mom during the day came into the room with him. He started to stand up.

"No, don't do that. Just sit there and eat. They've taken her away just as was arranged, Mr. Anderson. Also, because your mother was good about getting things taken care of, all the arrangements have been made too." He said he was aware of that. "Good, good. Also, there are just a couple of things for us to come back for. She wanted to donate the bed and equipment to us so we could get some use out of it. Such a fine woman, your mother."

"She was. Thank you. Yes, she told me last week that she was going to make sure you had what was left here. I'm to understand that everything that was left will be reused." She told him that was what his mom had wanted. "Good. I know she's made a donation to Hospice, too, in her will. I don't know what it would be, but

I'll make sure you have plenty for the help you give."

"Thank you, sir. We do appreciate yours and your mother's kindness." Nodding, he waited for her to leave or say something more. It was like this every time he spoke to the woman—she just didn't seem to know how to end a conversation. Even his mom had gotten a good giggle out of it. Finally, she left them, and he looked at Mary.

"You're to say something at the funeral." He said he'd gone over it with his mom yesterday. "She would have wanted you to say what was in your heart. And your mind. I'm going to have a nice spread here when the funeral is over. Bring back whoever would like to come. We'll make it work."

"I will make the announcement after my speech."

He got up, knowing he had a lot of things to do today. Avoiding the parlor where his mom had been staying, he made his way to his office. Caleb had left a great deal unfinished when he'd stopped everything to be with her.

Caleb had loved his mother more than he thought anyone had in all the children he'd met when he was younger. She'd taken the time to show him things he doubted any other parent had done. He knew how to trade stocks and make himself a good meal that didn't come out of a microwave. Caleb also had a good education and was at the top of his game in architectural design, both for the building he might be working on as well as the landscaping surrounding it. He had literally followed in her footsteps when it came to making a living.

"Sir? There is a man here to see you. I'm sorry, but he'd only tell me that he had an appointment with you." Caleb looked at his calendar and saw that, like he had thought, nothing was there. "Shall I send him on his way?"

"Yes. Tell him we're a house of mourning and don't have time for his shenanigans today. Thanks, Ben."

Caleb went back to work after smiling a little smile at him. Ben would enjoy sending the man on his way more than warranted, Caleb thought.

It was nearly dark when he finally lifted his head from work. He'd been behind, something he detested, but he wouldn't have changed things one bit if he had it to do over. Spending the last few days of his mom's life with her had been hard, but it had also been something they both needed. A time to say goodbye.

He went to the parlor first. The room was devoid of anything pertaining to the last days of his mom's life. The bed, as well as all the equipment, was now gone. The couch and chair that had sat in the room prior to being a sick room were now back in place. She would have wanted it done like this. Moving on. Mom had said that to him at least ten times a day when she'd been ill.

Going to the kitchen, he thanked Mary for what she'd done for them. Bursting into tears once again, he was glad for the warm hug from her. She sat him down, feeding him more than he thought he could have eaten, yet he finished every bite while she spoke to him.

"The director called here. I told him you were resting. I know you well enough to see that you working is almost the same as you getting a good eight hours of sleep. Did you get a lot done, Caleb?" He told her he thought he was caught up for now. "Good. She would have wanted that. Getting back to life now that hers is over. My goodness, I will miss that woman. She had a way about her that made a person wonder where she'd been all their life. And now that she was around them, well, they had a friend for life."

"She even told me which suit to wear at the funeral. And to wear one of her button roses on my lapel." He laughed a little. "I don't know what I'm to do without her. If she were here right now, she'd smack me in the back of the head and tell me I know just what to do and to get on with it. Mary, I'm not sure what to do, to be honest."

"You keep doing what she wanted of you." Mary got up and began cleaning the already spotless kitchen. "She called me to her room the other day. Asked me to stay on here until you got your feet under you. I'm not sure you ever had them under you all the way, but I'll stay until you decide on what you're going to do. She also said you'd marry soon. I didn't have a comment for that. I was not aware you'd been dating."

"I was until recently." He thought of Violet and shook his head. "I don't think she's going to be happy with me. I've decided she's not the woman for me. She told me she couldn't live here with me after having a death in the house. Like I had asked her to or something. No. She didn't even come here to sit with me when

Mom was in her last days. Told me she had more important things to do than to watch someone die. I thought that was very telling. What would she have done had it been me, I had to wonder? Do you think she might have gone shopping?"

They both laughed, and it felt good. Laughter had been encouraged within the walls of this house, and he'd missed it a great deal since his mom had been diagnosed with cancer. Mary told him he was to call the director back and to do it now. He was headed to the living room when he called, and it was answered on the first ring.

"I'm sorry it's so late, Mr. Carroll. I got into things here and didn't think you might need something from me. What can I help you with?" He told him that his mother was ready, did he want to see her before the funeral. Did he? Caleb wasn't sure but said he'd be there in the morning. "What time can I come in? I don't want to disturb your household."

"I'll have to have the little ones off to school by nine, sir. That should be enough time for you to get your hugs if you were to come by at eight-thirty." Caleb said he'd very much like that. "Good. I'll tell Margaret. She'll have them fed by then. They're as sorry as the rest of us are about her passing. She was a wonderful woman, your mom. Didn't take on like she was better than anyone when you needed a shoulder to cry on or even a little lift up. I don't know that I should be saying this to you, but you couldn't have had a better role model or mom than her, Caleb."

"I know. I thank my lucky stars all the time that she decided to keep me. I think we were very good for each other." He felt his eyes fill with tears again and wondered if there would ever be a time when he didn't want to sob when he thought of his mom being gone. "I'll see the family in the morning then. And then see to my mom. I'm sure you did an amazing job, Mr. Carroll."

After closing the connection, he headed up to his room. Caleb had lived in this house all his life except for the few years he'd gone off to college. Even then, he'd been home weekends and holidays. The two of them, with Mary and Ben, had had such good times together. When they vacationed, Mary and Ben had gone as well.

Making sure his suit was clean, he pulled out the shirt his mother had picked out for him too. Smiling, he wondered what everyone would think about it. He was positive that no one would expect him to wear a pink paisley shirt with a suit. But that was what his mom wanted, and he was going to do this one thing, the last thing he could for her, without any qualms about it.

Closing his eyes after stripping down, he wasn't sure he could sleep. But almost as soon as his head hit the pillow, he was out. He knew his alarm would go off well after he was up, and if not, then it would wake him to get started on his day. Caleb was nothing if not organized.

The next morning, he was up and ready to head out the door by a quarter to eight. Excited to see the kids, he stopped by the store to pick up a few things for them. Yes, he did spoil them, but they were his god children, and he loved them to pieces.

Sharon met him at the door with a stern look on her face. She was the most adult eight-year-old he'd ever met. "You brought us stuff, didn't you?" He handed her one of the wrapped gifts he'd picked up for her. "Your momma would bust your ears if she knew you were doing this. She said you spoil us too much."

"Yes, but she was just jealous that she

didn't spoil you as much as I did." She grinned at him. "I've missed you, Sharon. You and Paul. My mom thought about you often while she was ill."

"I'm gonna miss her too. She was the best grandma in the world." Sharon hugged him tightly around his neck when he bent to her level. Picking her up, he carried her into the kitchen, where her brother was still eating. "Paul, you were supposed to be done eating by now. How are you gonna give Caleb hugs when you're covered in mush?"

"I've dressed for the occasion. Come here, Paul. Give me a big hug."

After getting his hugs, the kids ran off when he handed them the other gifts he'd gotten. Making sure they knew they needed to come to him before they left for school, he settled down with Margaret and Paul.

"I've done as she asked. My goodness, I do love her choice of her sending-off outfit. Your mom, she wasn't one on doing what others did, was she?" Caleb laughed, knowing that his mother had picked out an outfit that would not just shock but would make people laugh. It was what she had wanted. "If you'd like to see her after the children have gone, I can take you there. The service will be in the large chapel. I've also been receiving a few flowers."

"There won't be a notice in the paper. The people that need to know have been notified. That's the way she wanted it." Wilson nodded. "She'll be happy with the way things are going. I plan on doing just what she wanted. Because knowing her as well as I do, she really will come back and smack me on the back of the head if I don't."

"She was a good woman, that mother of yours." Margaret handed him a framed photo of the two of them. "I never saw a woman so determined to make sure she was successful after having you. Abby wanted only the best for you and her after being tossed out. It's a small wonder she didn't want her parents notified in the paper. They didn't deserve anyone like her as their daughter. Nor you as their grandson."

"I'm to tell them in person." Neither one of them said anything after he made his announcement. "She told me it has to be done in person and that I wasn't to allow them to say anything to me about how she was a terrible child. There is a letter with our attorney that she wrote in her final days. If they refuse to read it, then I'm to read it to them, so they understand what sort of person she was. Do you suppose they would have kept up with her life after her leaving home?"

"I wouldn't think so. Abby wouldn't have been one to let them into her life after she was tossed aside, either. Have you heard from her brother? What was his name?" He told Margaret. "That's it. Sheppard. What a piece of shit he was too. Even before Abby left home, he was a mean little prick."

"Margaret." She huffed at Paul when he scolded her. "We need to keep a civil tone with this. For all we know, they wanted to contact her but weren't sure how to go about it."

"Doubtful. I knew them before this happened, so I'm in a position to tell you they weren't nice people at all." Margaret went to get the children, as it was time for the bus. "Mark my words, Caleb. When push comes to shove, you push them back as hard as you can. They don't deserve any sympathy at all for what they did."

After hugging the children, he made his way to the lower level to make sure that Mom was just the way she'd wanted. There were a lot of things in the room, including flowers that indicated that a donation had been made in the deceased's honor. Mom looked to him as if she'd fallen asleep and was resting peacefully. It hurt him again how much he was going to miss her.

"You got her hair and makeup just perfect, Mr. Carroll. And the shirt is perfect for my mom. She bought this about four years ago when we were in Hawaii." Carroll said something, but Caleb was thinking about that vacation. "She found a way to work with some of the beautiful shells that were in abundance around the island. I think she must have put three or four kids through college with that venture."

"I've seen those houses. If I remember correctly, they were featured on the cover of a few magazines as well." He nodded and turned from the casket. "You're going to be just fine, Caleb. You're your mother's son, and you'll gather strength where you least expect it, I'm thinking."

Nodding, he left. There wasn't much he could say to that. Caleb went home to work again and found that he could bury himself in work, and the pain would lessen. He was nearly finished working for the day when Mr. Fowler, their attorney, called to ask him if he needed anything.

"Nothing I can think of. I'm assuming you're wanting to get her will taken care of." He said there was no hurry. "Thank you for that. But there are a few things you have for me that I need to take care of after the funeral. Mom said you have the addresses."

"I do. Wasn't hard to find them. Mr. and Mrs. Anderson still live in the same house. I only had to read the paper to see where her brother was. Nasty piece of work, him. Anyway, it's all here. Just tell me when you want to go, and I'll go with you. You are taking me, right?" That was what his mom had wanted in the event they tried to hurt him. "Also, there are some envelopes here for Mary and Ben and for the children of Mr. Carroll. I'm assuming she paid for them to go to college as she had mentioned before."

"I don't know, to be honest. She didn't want me to know all her plans. Mom said it would spoil the surprise. I'm not sure what she meant by that, but I guess it'll be all right." Gus laughed a little. "If you could bring it to the funeral home tomorrow, I'll take care of it after the reception at the house. If you have time to go then?"

"I've only worked for your family for years, Caleb. Watched you grow into a good man too. No, you tell me when and I'll be there with bells on." Thanking him, Caleb decided that if he could, he was going to keep Gus on until he was too tired to work for him. Almost as if he had read his mind, Gus spoke again. "Also, you might want to know that I've been looking into a replacement. I know you and your mother have paid me well for all these years, but you need someone younger than this eighty-year-old geriatric. My granddaughter would be good for you or her brother. Might need them both after a while. But I've told them all they need to know about your plans, as well as your money. Who would have thought that when your mom came to see me, fat with her baby boy, that she'd be one of the richest women in the world? She certainly did work for it. So have you."

Caleb went to bed that night, knowing he had to be on his best game tomorrow. It was going to be a long day, and he wasn't sure how well he was going to handle it. But he also knew that in some way, his mom was watching over him, so he was up for the challenge. At least he hoped he was.

The next morning, he was at the funeral home at a little past seven. Hugging the kids again gave him strength and love. They were not going to school today, he'd found out, so they could be there for their parents. It was going to be a big funeral, and all hands were needed. Caleb thought that having them where he could grab a hug or two was going to be just the thing. Kids, he knew, had an understanding of grief that went well beyond their years on this earth.

When everyone was seated that there were chairs for, a great many people standing around the room, he went to the podium and cleared his throat. It was time, he thought. A microphone had been unearthed so the people in the long hall leading to the chapel could hear him.

"I noticed that a few of you got a kick out of the way we're dressed. You know Mom. When there was a gathering of people, she wanted to party." Another round of laughter, and he pulled out his notes. "My mom approved my speech that I'm going to give today. I also want you to know that while I was writing this, she was checking my spelling, as well as looking for any grammatical errors. She knew I'd have it all wrong if she didn't.

"My mom was seventeen when she was tossed out of her family home. Again, this is her story, not mine. Her parents decided it was shameful to have an unwed daughter around when she began to show. Not to mention, according to her father, she was spoiled for all other men after that, whatever that meant to him. Then, when I was born, she sent a telegram telling her family of my birth. That she had had a healthy baby boy and that we were both doing fine."

Looking at his notes, he continued. "After my birth, Mom made sure she could support not only herself but me as well. After getting her high school diploma with me at her feet sleeping, she got into college and then got a job." Caleb almost skipped over some of the notes but went back to them. "While she worked and studied, Mom taught me what hard work and determination could afford a person. It's a lesson I've taken with me all my life and will continue to do so." He knew this next part was going to be the hardest to say.

"Several months ago, after finding out she was beyond help with the diagnoses of cancer, she began making plans that would be felt by the rest of the town we call home for the entirety of its future." There were a few murmurs of wonder, but he ignored them. "I've decided it would be in all our best interests if I should carry on my mom's legacy and continue to support the causes we have before."

Before sitting down, Caleb announced that there would be a reception with light food at his home. Going to his seat, he watched as the funeral director took his place and announced that there was a nice luncheon at the Anderson home. Then he asked people to go to their cars. He'd said all he wanted to say at the funeral home.

At the reception, people came to wish him well and to tell him how sorry they were for his loss. Caleb wanted to tell them that sorry didn't bring her back to him, but he didn't. His grief was profound. The finality of what they were doing here hurt him deeply in his soul and heart.

People came to speak to him about his mom, telling stories that they knew about her that he knew as well. There was one that he so enjoyed thinking about. It was about when Mom had come upon a child in one of the barns, crying because her cat was going to die. The little thing was in hard labor, and the kitten was turned the wrong way. After assisting in the birth after resolving the issue, Mom stuck around for the rest of the birthing.

"Then, not two weeks later, Mr. Jamison calls her up and tells your mom that he has a cow in a bad way. Not sure why he'd think she could help, your mom, being her, she went there and helped with the birth of that cow. Mr. Jamison, he named the calf after her, and to this day, he refers to it as Abigail when asked. Darnest thing I done ever did see, I tell you." Mr. March laughed and acted like that was the only time his mom had gone out on an emergency like the ones with the cow and kittens. "I heard tell she was there when Mrs. Parker gave birth to those twin little boys too."

There were many stories like that one. Mom had driven the school bus one week when the system had been short-staffed. She'd helped bring in some crops, driving the big tractor like she'd been born to it. He loved all of them, even the ones told about when he was an infant.

Mr. Fowler caught up with him just as people were beginning to leave. As they entered his office, he was sure he was going to tell him something he didn't want to hear. Gus told him he'd not be able to go with him in the morning, as something else had come up.

"I'm to be acting county judge tomorrow. The one that was coming here to hear some of the backed-up cases got himself a case of food poisoning, from his mother-in-law, of all people. Anyway, they didn't really ask so much as told me that it was my duty as a good standing attorney to see to this. I'm hoping it's a one-time shot, but who knows what will happen with all this other stuff going on." Caleb said he could go when he was finished. "No. I've spoken to my grandchildren. They're good, Caleb, if not a little green on things. They're ready to go with you to keep you out of hot water if things go badly there."

Caleb did want to get this over with and move on. When Gus handed him the things he'd need when he went to confront his mom's parents—never would they be his grandparents, he thought—he decided to go.

"I'll go, but I don't like it. I wasn't even sure I was onboard with it when I thought you were going with me." Gus said he was sorry.

"Not as sorry as they'll be if I have to get into it with them. But you are right. I need to get this finished so I can focus on my life without my mom. I knew she was dying, Gus, but it's hard for me to realize she's gone. I find myself looking for her or even going into the parlor when I think of something I want to say to her. I wonder if it will ever get better."

"Yes. It'll soften after a while, the pain of it. When my Marie passed on, it was all I could do to get myself cleaned up and fed daily." He laughed a little. "Your mom did a fine job of shaking me around a little. But she was good to do that. Not only did she save my life — I'll believe that forever — but she got me moving in the right direction to keep my sanity as well. That mom of yours, Caleb, she knew how to make a person see her way about things."

"She was the best." Gus agreed with him, and Caleb smiled. "I'll take both of them with me tomorrow. That way, they can show me that they can work with someone like me. Someone who is a little too demanding at times but means well."

"Yes, well, I don't think you're demanding at all, but a man that likes to get things going.

Also, before I forget, once you're back, we'll go over your mom's will. There are a couple of things she added in the final few days. Some of it you'll need to care for." Caleb asked him if he needed to take care of them now. "No. nothing like that. But just some things she had for you. I'll see you when you return, Caleb. You do what your mom asked, and that'll hopefully be the end of it."

After getting a file from his car regarding the family, Gus left. Kylie and Arthur were to meet Caleb here at his house at seven sharp. It wasn't a far trip to make, a couple of hours of driving time, but since he was driving, he didn't want anyone to make him late.

Chapter 2

Tabby hated waiting. When she'd been summoned here—well, a police officer had shown up at her door at eight this morning—she knew it was going to be a long day. Whatever they had to say, she wanted them to say it so she could go job hunting again. The fucking shithead she worked for wasn't going to get the better of her.

"You say you gave your notice, Miss Tillman?" She said, for the fourth time, that she had. "I'm sorry, but this is all new to me. Shep said you didn't show up to work this morning and that he'd told you he had an important meeting you had to attend with him."

Mr. Anderson was as dumb as his son was a fucking prick if he thought Shep ever went to meetings. She'd been running the flipping company since the day she'd been hired. Then when she'd found out that there had been bonuses given to Shep from the company, six figures kind of bonuses, she got so pissed off she gave her notice and left. Shep had a great deal to answer for.

"There are several meetings that had been set up for Shep, Mr. Anderson. However, it's doubtful he would have shown up to any of them. He rarely comes into work before noon and leaves not long after, having a four or five hour lunch. I'm not telling tales here, but I can't work his job and mine and not get the perks that he is." When the front doorbell chimed, she, as well as Mr. and Mrs. Anderson, turned to it. After the butler let the three people in, she turned back to Mr. Anderson. "This is all water under the bridge, sir. I've given my notice, and I no longer work for him, nor you. If you want my advice, I'd fire his ass and find someone that will actually do a day's work for you."

"Well, I don't want your advice. Shep has been, according to the information I've been receiving, doing a good job." He looked at the people in the doorway, and she did as well. "I don't know what you're selling, but I've no time for it today. Go by the offices and —"

"I'm here about your daughter, Abigail Anderson." Mr. Anderson paled as his wife held onto him for what looked like much-needed support. "I see you remember her. I'd like only a few minutes of your time, then I'll be on my way."

"What is the meaning of this? My daughter hasn't lived here for a great many years." The stranger told him it had been twenty-seven years, give or take a few months. "What do you want? Money? I don't work with blackmailers. You be on your way before I call the police."

"She died six days ago." Mr. Anderson nearly hit the floor and would have if not for the other man holding him up. "Where is a good place for you to sit down? You're looking a little pole axed if you ask me."

"How do you know this?"

The man took the couple into the dining room when it was pointed out. Tabby went along too. There was plenty to get finished on her end, and she wasn't going to let them scoot her under the rug now that she was here. There was also the matter of her last check, as well as her vacation pay coming to her.

She'd been willing to let it go, but now that they'd brought her here, she was going to bitch about it. However, right now, she wanted to find out about this man and his entourage. Also, about the daughter she'd never heard of. Shep joined them in the dining room just as the man started talking.

"What's all this about? Tabitha, shouldn't you be at work slaving away? I know for a fact that your calendar is quite full today." He sat down, and a large plate of food was brought to him. It looked like eggs and bacon. "Ah yes. The most important meal of the day. Breakfast."

"It's nearly noon now, Shep. Why did you tell me that Miss Tillman didn't give you notice?" Shep waved his father off, and she thought that was the end of it. But Mr. Anderson looked at the stranger then. "I didn't catch your name."

Instead of giving him what he wanted, the man handed him a letter. There was a file set before the man, but he didn't do anything more than shove it in her direction. Taking it, she opened it to the first page and saw Shep's picture there. She was going through the file when the young woman that had come with Stranger man sat down beside her. Leaning in, she whispered in her ear.

"I'm to help you." She asked her what with. "Your dealings with the younger Anderson. We know that Sheppard Anderson the fourth has been taking advantage of you in different ways. Sexually harassing you by cornering you in parts of the buildings. Also, in business dealings in which you've taken over most of the daily running of the plant. My boss there said you should be running the entire thing and would be if he had anything to do about it."

They spoke quietly while the older couple read the letter that had been in the envelope the young woman's boss had turned over to them. Shep reached for the file Tabby was going over. She didn't see the stranger move. Not only was Shep on the floor, but he had his arm pulled up behind his back with his thumb pulled up tightly to his wrist.

"Did she say you could touch her things?" Shep started cursing the moment the man spoke. "No, she didn't, in the event you were going to say something differently. Those are her things that she was given. At no time did anyone say you could look at it."

"Who the fuck are you? And why the hell are you in my house?" Mr. Anderson said it was his house until he said differently. "Whatever. What the hell is he doing in your house then?"

"Shep, I'd like for you to meet your nephew, Caleb Anderson." Mr. Anderson started to cry a little. "You look so much like her that it hurts my heart a little for all the things we did and have lamented for years."

Mrs. Anderson stood up, but when she went to Caleb, he backed away from her as she approached him. Putting her hand to her mouth, she nodded only once before speaking to him.

"I deserve that. And so much more. But I do hope you'll give us a chance now that you're here. We made a great many mistakes with Abby. So many I'm sure she didn't tell you about." He said she'd told him only they were her parents, and they'd tossed her aside when she was going to have him. "I would have thought that— No. Not Abby. She'd not do that no matter how we treated her. No, I can see her only telling you what you needed to know."

"She asked me to come here and to hand you this letter." He finally let go of Shep. The older man stood, but Caleb towered over him.

Shep backed away. "I've some information on your son as well that I think you need—"

"They know all about my shit, little nephew. So, my sister went and kept you. Biggest mistake she's ever made, I would imagine." Shep looked Caleb up and down before he snorted. "Not much to you, is there?"

Had she not been looking at both men, she would have missed it. Caleb's fist connected with Shep's chin in a hard quick blow that had the older man falling to the floor, breaking a chair as well as hitting his head on the broken dish that had been in his hand. Tabby started laughing hard enough to draw unwanted attention to herself.

"I have wanted to do that for the last few months. Your son, I'm sorry to tell you, is a fucking asshole." She stood up when Kylie did. "I'm going to get my last check that he threatened to hold from me, as well as all my vacation time that I couldn't take because he never showed up at the office."

"Yes, of course, you will." Startled, Tabby looked at Mr. Anderson. "I've seen enough over the last few hours that I'm sure we can figure something out. Also, if you'd not quit just yet, young lady, I'd like to speak to you." Tabby sat back down, feeling like a yo-yo when Kylie did the same thing. "Shep, I'd like a few words with you. Abby has pointed out a few things in her letter that I think you have been up to without regard to how it affects everyone around you."

Tabby didn't care for all this. She had things she had to do. Like finding herself a job. Even if she had to take a pay cut with the next one, she'd be ahead since she'd never been paid overtime — even when it was promised — nor had she gotten paid for the number of real hours she had put in. She looked over at Kylie when she said her name quietly.

"If he offers you the job, would you take it?" She asked her what job she was talking about. "The one you've been doing all along. Running the business that Shep has pretty much abandoned. He will offer it to you. He's seen the work you've done. That was given to him earlier this morning. I faxed it to him when I knew you were here."

"How did you know I was going to be here when I didn't?" Kylie told her. "I see. So, my nosey neighbors told you what was going on. There are days when they know more about my life than I think I do. You came here to help me out of this mess. Why?"

"Mr. Anderson—since you know his name now, I can refer to him that way—had been reading over the paperwork that my grandfather had given him while we drove here. He said that you were getting a bum deal out of this and asked me if I'd like to have a chance to help you out." Tabby asked her why she'd taken her on. "Caleb is a good man, Tabby. His mom was a great woman who taught her son that to not help would be the same as being the cause of a situation. Me helping you is making sure that things are done properly for not just you in this case, but the other twenty or so women and some men that Shep has been abusing with the same thing you've experienced. The nonpayment of overtime is a biggy."

There were some harsh words said as both the Anderson men spoke. Caleb didn't say much, only answering questions when they were put to him. Tabby admired Caleb for what he was doing.

Not knowing the people he was related to must have been hard on him, especially since his mom had only just passed away. But he'd done as he said he would and came here to give the couple a letter from his mom. Not only that, but Tabby had an idea he'd saved her a great deal of pain when he'd flipped Shep to the floor. Shep had a tendency to hit first then walk away rather than hearing anything he didn't want to. It was the reason she avoided him unless absolutely necessary, especially when it came to work problems. She looked at Shep when he said her name.

"You're going to take the word of a daughter you fucking kicked out and that of Tabby, an employee that was quitting, over me?" Mr. Anderson looked at her before answering his son that he thought she was more truthful. "Dad, you have no idea the kind of crap I have to put up with from her every day. She's forever trying to do shit to my company that I have to go in and undo. Giving raises to herself. Tabby even had the vending people come in and put in another machine that I didn't approve, going so far as to signing a five-year contract with them so I couldn't undo it. But I will, you mark my words on that shit."

"Did you do it for the good of the employees, Tabitha?" She told him there wasn't anything left in the other machines by the end of the first lunch. Tabby told him she would have put in three more if the company had them in stock. "Good for you. The way to a good company, I've come to realize, is to have good people backing you up. I'm assuming you didn't give yourself a raise."

"No. I haven't even gotten the pay I was promised when I started doing his job. It took me three nights of working past everyone else to get all the crap off his desk and into some kind of order." He nodded and looked at Shep. "Mr. Anderson, I've never done anything that was a benefit to me. All I've done is make the decisions he wouldn't. My mom works there, and she told me what he was doing with the money from the vending machines."

"Christ, is this grade school? Are you going to tattle on me about my bathroom schedule too?" She told Shep she didn't know his schedule since he didn't show up for work all that often. "Why, you fucking bitch."

Again, the movement was quick. One moment Shep was leaping toward her, then the next he was simply gone. When she stood up and looked over the table, Shep was sprawled out all over the floor with a bloodied nose and lip. Caleb didn't look like his part in the laying out of Shep had harmed him in any way. He looked at her, Kylie, and Arthur and asked if they were ready for lunch. Before they knew it, both Mr. and Mrs. Anderson were joining them.

This was the strangest thing she'd been witness to in her life. Everyone simply just stepped over Shep as they made their way to the front door. The butler that had shown her to the room had been instructed to get Shep out and to have someone come and change the locks. And just like that, Shep was forgotten.

~*~

Caleb watched the two women with them. Kylie was forever bending her head to Tabby's and smiling. Whatever they were plotting, he had a feeling it wasn't going to bode well for Shep. Not that he cared. The man was a putz. More than that, he was a prick too.

"May I ask you some things about Abby?" He looked at Mrs. Anderson and told her he would answer them truthfully. "I'd not expect anything less, I don't think. You've proven yourself to be a very effective force when you need to be. But Abby. What did she do for a living? For that matter, what do you do now?"

"Mom studied to be a designer. Mostly it was for her to learn how to use a sewing machine, but she liked designing homes. Then the landscaping aspect of it. She became an architect when she realized there were few women in the business. I have a doctorate in architecture, as well as lawn care and design. We formed our own company about five years ago. It's something she could do anywhere and anytime, so it made it simple for us to vacation and work as well." She asked him if he had any pictures of her creations. Pulling out his phone, he showed her the project they'd been working on when she'd gotten sick. "It's finished now, of course. When she was resting or seeing the doctor, I'd go there and work with the men building. It's the home of the artist that does the amazing paintings outside of the city where we live." She thumbed through the pictures as he kept an eye on Arthur and Kylie.

They were out of their element, he knew, but he did engage them in conversation when he could. Tabby was keeping up a steady flow of conversation with them as well. Caleb wasn't entirely sure what he was supposed to say to the couple that was his grandparents. He'd never had any before and didn't know how to interact with them at all.

"Would she have been upset?" He looked at Mrs. Anderson. "About us having lunch with you. I know we barged in on your plans. Sheppard didn't ask, but I'm ever so glad you didn't turn us away."

"Mom being mad? Not likely. She didn't get angry often. Mom told me it was a total waste of time. And it didn't get you anywhere but in a bad mood. There were times when she'd be spitting mad at something or someone, but she'd write them a note and then burn it. It was the way she dealt with stress as well." Mrs. Anderson showed him one of the pictures of the two of them together. "We were on a cruise that year. I think to Alaska. She started getting ill after we returned home, and that was when we found out she had cancer."

"We missed so much." Caleb said they had. "You really don't pull any punches, do you? I find it refreshing, I think. A little rude, but that's fine too. I'm sure you've been taught that we're monsters for what we did to her."

"No, I was told nothing but that you were

her parents. She didn't even talk about the three of you too much when she was dying, just about the things we'd done together. There were times when I'd ask her about you, little things about how you could have hurt her so much. She'd tell me that you had hurt her, but she'd been able to be with me, and that made it so worthwhile." Mrs. Anderson nodded and continued to look through his pictures. "Mom wanted me to have a relationship with you. She never told me I had to or what sort of relationship she'd like for me to pursue. However, she did tell me I was to go to see you with this letter and to keep an open mind and head. I don't know what I want from either of you, to be honest. I have money, a great deal of it. I have several businesses that I work with. You have very little that I think I want or need. I don't mean to be cruel, but I've made it this far in my life, and I more than likely will continue to do the same thing whether you are a part of it or not."

"Caleb, you *are* being rude, and you know it." He looked at Tabby and smiled. "I'm not going to tell you to tell your grandmother you're sorry, but I think you do need to lighten up a little. There is a time and a place for being blunt, and I don't think this is it. All right?"

"Yes, ma'am." Looking back at Mrs. Anderson, he said he was sorry. "However, I did tell you I wouldn't hold back on answers. I know I was rude, and I'm sorry for that. I'll be better now." He looked at Tabby. "Does that get me out of the doghouse with you?"

"I'm not sure. I have been meaning to thank you for having Kylie help me. I guess that was my way of breaking the ice with you." He said he'd like to think he was approachable. "Perhaps you are, Mr. Anderson. However, I'm not even close to being in your neck of the woods, from what I can tell, and I did want to thank you."

"I have no idea what you mean by that, but I'm just a man who just happens to have some money. If that is what's putting you off and having you call me Mr. Anderson, then I'd like to note that you call Shep by his first name, and I'm not nearly the ass he is." She cleared her throat and looked in the direction of Mrs. Anderson. "I'm sure she knows her son is an ass, Tabby. I do believe they've both known it a good deal longer than I was made aware of."

"Your mother would smack you upside the head, I think." Caleb laughed and decided that he liked this woman for her ability to call him on the carpet yet still call him mister. "I'm just saying I'm sure you have women falling at your feet all the time, and I'd just be a notch on your headboard."

"Doubtful that you'd allow anyone to get that close to you and let them think you were some kind of conquest. No. I see you as the type of woman that knows what her worth is and doesn't let the opinions of others stand in her way when she wants something." Mr. Anderson agreed with him. "She could do a damned sight better job of running your company, Mr. Anderson, than the man you have working there now. Shep, judging from what I've read up on your company on the way here, is going to fail soon."

"That is what I wanted to talk to her about. Your attorney there, Miss Fowler, faxed me a great deal of paperwork yesterday afternoon and into this morning. I was going over it when you showed up. It was what I brought Tabby to my house to discuss with her. Or, at the time, it was to tell me what she was doing hiring a lawyer to lie to me about my son. But I've come to realize the same thing you did in a shorter amount of time. Miss Tillman is the person I want to run my company. I'm sure she'd do a better job if I give her control than she's been doing behind my son's back."

"I can't do that. It's a multibillion-dollar company." Mr. Anderson pointed out to her that she'd been doing it. "Well, yes, I guess I have, but if it all went belly up, then I could walk away."

"You wouldn't have done that. Walk away, I mean." Caleb looked at Mrs. Anderson when she spoke up. He asked her what she meant. "Two things before I answer that. Since I'm sure you're not going to call me Grandma, will you please stop calling me Mrs. Anderson? I'm Melissa. My husband is Sheppard. Second thing, the company was mine before I married Sheppard. And we, as a couple, make all decisions concerning it and how it is run. The only disagreement we've had in it was letting Shep run things. That was a mistake I'll not make again. But Sheppard is correct. Tabby could run the place like a dream if she were to be given the reins of it."

"She is owed a great deal of backpay, Mr. and Mrs. Anderson." This time it was Arthur who spoke. "Not an insignificant amount either. Over the last few months alone, she's managed to get in about seventy-plus hours a week while only getting paid for half that. Her vacations were canceled, and Shep, your son, managed to get into her 401K account and take about half of that from her. It's a very sticky situation Tabby is in. And one that could, if taken to court, result in—"

"No. I don't want to go to court if they're willing to pay me what I'm owed for my vacation money. I have lost a great deal of money on deposits that I was unable to get back too." Caleb asked Tabby what Shep had said when she didn't get her deposit back after canceling her vacations. "That I should know better than to schedule a vacation I couldn't get my deposit back on. Jerk."

He laughed when her face turned red. "He sounds like a person I knew in college. Forever wanting things his way. He didn't do a lick of work nor show up to classes. So, when graduation day came around, his name, of course, wasn't on the list of people in the ceremony." He laughed a little more before speaking again. "He went to the bursar and told him that he'd invited a great many people to his graduation. The man told him they could hang around and wait if they wanted, but it would more than likely be another four or so years. No amount of begging or threatening could get the man to change his mind. And rightly so. Too many people want to skate along on someone else's coattails and think that's all right. Not all of them are bad people. Some of them more than likely didn't know it was wrong since they'd gotten away with it as a young person. Or learned it from their parents. Whatever made them into what they became, it was from something that worked for them, and they used it."

"Are those people redeemable, you think?" Caleb said the problem would be if the person wanted to be redeemed. Tabby nodded. "I think Shep could be redeemable. He's not stupid. Well, he could be about some things, but he could be taught. Or, and I think this is a biggie, shown that what he was doing wasn't just hurting the company, but the very people that made it so he had money in his pocket when he wanted it and a lovely home that he lived in. Well, I guess until recently. Do you think he could change?"

"I don't know him at all other than that he tried to bully you at the house." He watched her face as she thought about it. "I would guess the only person that knows would be him. And if he found a reason for wanting to change himself."

"I thought that was what we were doing when we gave him control of the office. He did steal from us when living at home. I thought he'd learn the value of money and that he'd be a better man for it." Melissa looked at Sheppard before turning back to him. "I was wrong on a great many things in my life. That is only one of them. I know it's too late for me to redeem myself with my daughter, and you've no idea how much I'd like to do that, but with you, I'd like to get to know you as much as you'll allow it, Caleb."

He'd been thinking about it too. Not what had happened, because he knew in his mom's plight of being thrown out, he didn't have all the details. But with these people. They'd changed, he'd bet. Not just in feeling sorry about what they'd done—again, not enough details to make a decision. Caleb did want to get to know them in a non-relationship way. Even though they were his grandparents and Shep, his uncle, he wasn't sure a relationship was possible. However, he wasn't closing the door simply because he could.

"I'd like that. I have a job that affords me to

live anywhere I wish. A home I love that I shared with my mom. Also, business situations that I simply cannot walk away from at the moment. But I will make it so that I can hang around this area for a little while. So long as you understand, this is as new to me as it is to the two of you. We have missed a great many years through no fault of my own, so I'd like to take it slowly." They both agreed, a little too quickly, he thought, but he was all right with that too for now. "I have to return to hear the reading of the will. Then I'll return. If it's all right with you, I'd like to leave Kylie and Arthur here so they can get things settled so I can come back and keep working. I'd need a place to work from. I do better with plenty of light. They'll have the specs on what I need before I leave."

"That's wonderful." He glanced at Tabby when she smiled. "Sorry. Just knowing I'll have someone in my corner with Kylie when it comes to getting things situated for my new job will be nice. I still have a job, don't I?"

"You do. And I'll work with you as well. Both Melissa and I will. We'll also work with Shep." Arthur said he'd help with him getting things worked up. Caleb wasn't sure what that meant, but he thought that if Arthur said he'd work on him, he'd do it. "Also, before you leave, Caleb, Melissa said you had a few pictures of your mom. I'd like to see them if you'd not mind."

"No, I don't mind. However, when I return, I'll bring back some of the photo albums that Mom put together. She enjoyed having printed pictures and putting them together with dates and such. I'll bring them back if you'd like to see them." He had to look away from them for a second. Their hope-filled eyes hurt him deep in his heart. "I need to get back today for an early appointment. If you need to get in touch with me for any reason, Kylie has that information that she can share with you."

After lunch, he made his way back to the car. He would take a plane when he came back, he thought. It was quicker, and he'd simply rent himself a car if needed. Things weren't progressing the way he'd envisioned them going, but he wasn't unhappy with the progress either. Time would tell, his mom used to say all the time. He had a full understanding of that statement as he drove himself back home.

Chapter 3

"Other than his name being Howard Berkley and that he's deceased, that's about all I have on him. While she asked me to look him up a few weeks before she passed on, there wasn't much to go on. It took me a dickens of a time to even figure out that he was dead." Caleb looked at the list of names that had been handed to him. "Those are the births that have his name on this as father. Again, a hard time finding them. But I got me a little helper at the courthouse, and she was glad to help me with this list."

"She wants me to find these other men." Gus told him that of those seven names minus his, there was one deceased young man. "So, I'm to find these other five men and do what with them? I know that technically they're my half-brothers, but other than that, I don't know them anymore than I do Mom's parents."

"Abby had it in her head that you could help them. I have done a little research on a couple of them, and she would have been correct on that score. Joey Phillips, like you, has lost his mom. She died some years ago from an automobile accident. Hit and run, and they've never found who did it. Also, Daniel Watson is in a bad way himself. Just last month, he was kicked out of his apartment for lack of payment. I've sent him some help already. I worry about him."

"Help them how, Gus? Send them money? I can do that easily. But I have a feeling that she has more in mind than just sending money to someone to get them out of a bad situation." Gus handed him a file that was as thick as anything he'd ever seen. "This is a lot of stuff here. Just give me the highlights, and I'll go over it later."

"What is it your mom told you about your conception?" Uncomfortable now, Caleb told the older man what had been told to him. "Drugged and then raped. Just as the other women had been. All of them conceived a child out of wedlock. Most of them weren't tossed aside as your mom was, but they had no less of a hard time. All the women were between the ages of seventeen and twenty and had a life before Howard Berkley came along and ruined them. Not my words, but those of a few people I was able to find that knew the man. The police didn't do anything about him, not even when these women came forward as a group."

"Mom wanted to help them through me." Gus nodded. "All right. I've never been able to say no to her, and I don't think now is a good time to start. So where is this Joey person? I'm sure you have enough information on him that I can hunt for him."

"I do. He's actually not far from here, about an hour's drive in the direction of Cincinnati. Joey had a job when he got out of the service, but that has since dried up. The place moved to another state, and while they offered employment to those that wanted it, there wasn't the means for him to be able to move. With the cost of the funeral he's still paying for, as well as trying to get his life back on track, it's making it difficult for him to make ends meet." Caleb looked at the picture of the other man. "I think you can see the resemblance between the two of you. Same eye color, as well as that dark hair. Your mom was a blonde, so you must have gotten it from him."

"Do you have a picture of him? This Berkley person?" He handed him a glossy 8x10, obviously a driver's license photo. Stuck to the back of it was another photo. "I have no idea why, but I didn't think he'd look this worn down. I figured for some reason he'd be a swagger-ish sort of man with dark curly hair and a mustache. He's a good deal older than I thought he'd be too."

"You have to remember that you were conceived twenty-seven years ago. He was only in his early thirties at the time. He may well have been swagger-ish back then. I heard from those that knew him that he was slick. A pedophile, of course, but he could charm the skin off a rattler if he wanted something. Since no one would go after him when it came to having him in jail, he continued his reign of terror throughout the area until he was killed one night in a bar fight. Another specialty of his. Drinking."

"And I'm related to this charming person." They both laughed, and he looked at the photo of the man. "Do you think it's possible that one or two of the women got tired of him and his ways and hired someone to kill him in the fight?

It would be something I'd do, I think."

"Possible. But I'm not going to lose any sleep over it. Are you?" He said he wasn't. "By the way, I've heard from the Andersons. They said they had some things of your mother's that they'd like to send here to you. Since I wasn't sure what it might be, I had them send it. I hope that is all right."

"Yes. I've packed up a few albums that Mom put together and am taking them back with me when I go there in a couple of days. Kylie is working with the Andersons indirectly through Tabby Tillman. I told you about her." Gus said she was a good person. "I hope so. I like her. And Kylie. Arthur is working out well with me. He's very quiet, which I like until he has all his ducks in a row, then he speaks. He has some good ideas for the business the Andersons have."

"I spoke to Kylie last night. She said Tabby has some good ideas for the place. I did a quick check on Anderson Diversified. They're a good company with some pots on the fire, so to speak. I think they could do much more, and from what Kylie was saying, they'll be making a good profit in no time. She's also hoping to bring morale up in the place." He asked if it had anything to do with Shep being gone. "I asked. She said that few people had ever seen him, so it wasn't like he was a big deal to them. However, Tabby was making a name for herself, I think, while she was running the organization."

"Good. She has the temperament for it. She reminds me a little of Mom in that she doesn't hold back when she has something on her mind. I really like that about her." Gus looked at him with a cocked brow. "Yes, all right? I really like her. She's calming to me in ways I've never realized I needed before. And she makes me laugh. The last few months hasn't had a great deal of anything to laugh about."

They spoke about a few other things in the will. Caleb received the bulk of the estate, and it was a huge one. Money went to the town for some things that Mom had been working on. Also, a scholarship had been set up for students that wished to go to college that didn't have the means. That meant, he thought, about anyone in their town. Also, she'd left enough money for the football stadium, as well as the field, to be overhauled. They had enjoyed a great many Friday nights at the local field, and she wanted to make sure the kids had new uniforms as well.

"What do you want me to do with the things she had in her safety deposit box? I'm not sure what would be in there after all this time, but the bank notified me that it was still sealed up." Caleb asked him if he could take care of it for him. "Yes. I just need you to sign the paperwork for me to go in as your power of attorney."

Signing off on that, he leaned back in his chair and regarded the other man. "You're not going to be my attorney anymore, are you?" Gus laughed and told him his mother would have been proud of him for being point-blank about it. "Don't stall, Gus. Are you enjoying being the judge? I'm to understand that you've been offered the position. You should take it."

"I've not decided just yet. I'm leaning toward it, to be honest with you. My missus, she would have been so proud had she been around. I'm finding it's not nearly as difficult as I thought it would be. I've been in this town long enough to know about every person that has a record, and then some." He laughed a little. "Besides, I think my grandkids would murder me if I were to come back to working with you. They're enjoying it very much. And Arthur was telling me that you already have him working on a couple of projects."

"He thinks outside the box." Gus told him he'd never done that. "Not true. You have done it, but Arthur, he is spinning wheels in his mind all the time, and I'm thinking he'll work well with me. Long term. I also see Kylie keeping him in line should he stew too long about anything. She's a marvel at Post-it notes. I bet she has stock in the company."

"She might well have. I like the way she organizes them, too—by importance by color. Arthur has a notebook that he carries around. I've never actually seen him use it, but he has it in his pocket with a number two pencil that I think he used in grade school."

They spoke about this and that. Nothing earth-shattering, but it was nice to bounce ideas off him about upcoming projects. Gus also told Caleb that the transfer of Kylie and Arthur being his attorneys from now on wouldn't cause any kind of ripple. Their names had been on his stationery for some time now.

"I suppose I should ask you about their pay, but I'm so happy with them that I don't care. I mean, I do, but they're worth it." Gus thanked him and said that Kylie's pay was being paid by the Andersons. "I guess since she now works with them, that it should be. Arthur is going to be paid by me, so you can set that up for me, right?"

"I can. Perks too?" He said for both of them if the Anderson's didn't provide them. "I believe they have, but I'll check into that. When do you leave?"

"The day after tomorrow. I have some things here in town that I need to see to. The building that Mom had started on before she got ill is finished and ready to be approved. I started working on the mockup before she passed away." He thought about not having his mom at the house. "The house isn't the same, Gus. It's too quiet and lonely. Every place I go in it, there is another jolt of memories that take me back. None of them are bad memories. Mom and I made a great many good ones in that house. But she's gone, and I can't stand the place anymore."

"You want to put it on the market?" He said he was thinking on it. "All right. Wherever you go, you know that Mary and Ben will go with you. Even though they could officially retire, I think they might enjoy new digs as well."

He was shaking his head before Gus finished. "I talked to Mary about it this morning. She said that with the money Mom left them, they're going to get them a home out west. Mary has some family out there, and she thought perhaps the weather would be good for Ben too." He thought about it for a moment. "If you'll have the things moved out of the house and put into storage, for now, I'll have it put on the market. I'm not sure where I'll live for the moment, but I'll find something."

He thought about the houses he'd seen where the Andersons lived and dismissed that. Living near them might be what they wanted, but Caleb was still coming to terms with things, and he wasn't going to make a long-term commitment until he figured things out.

After getting things set up for the move, he decided he'd had enough excitement for one day. Heading home, he thought about the projects here that were ongoing and realized none of them required him to live in the town he'd grown up in for them to be finished. He found himself by the apartment complex he and his mother had lived in when she'd been going to college, and he'd been nothing more than a kid.

The place had been condemned about five years ago. When they'd been living there, he remembered all kinds of things that were wrong with the apartment the two of them were in. Windows were broken, and plastic had been put over them. There hadn't been any air conditioner either, so having the broken window had served them well, he supposed. One burner on the stove had been a pain, but his mom had made it an adventure. Everything with her had been something of an adventure.

"I miss you so much, Mom." Pulling out of the drive, he made his way home. "I'm going to have myself a journey, I think. I'm going to go out to your parents' house, get to know them, and then work from there. I have no idea what that might bring to me, and right now, I don't know that I care all that much. I'm going to let myself flow with the current. And if I don't care for this one, I'm sure I can think about getting myself into another one fairly quickly."

Caleb was excited now, more so than he'd been in some time. Going into the house, he saw Mary in the living room and hugged her tightly. When he moved back from her, she looked up at him with both surprise and love.

"I'm putting the house on the market." She smiled at him and told him she thought that was a very good idea. "I have them on occasion. Also, I'm going to have everything put into storage. I want you and Ben to take whatever it is you want. I've only just decided to start fresh someplace. Anything and everything is up for grabs."

"My goodness, that's a change from the young man that left here this morning. What got into you? Not that I mind — it sure would be nice to have some of the things here, if you're sure." He told her that he was positive. "Then we'll go through it. I'm so proud of you, Caleb. I know your mother would be as well. She wanted this for you. To get on with your life."

"I miss her terribly, but staying here, I won't be able to move on. I think this house holds too many memories for me to go out and make my own." He wiggled his brows at her. "Not to mention, I might get myself laid faster if I don't have to travel so far to my bed."

"Go on you." She smacked him on the arm, and he laughed with her. "Met someone, have you? What's she like? Will I approve?"

"I don't know if I've met that someone yet. But I do like this woman named Tabby." He'd been thinking about her a great deal since he'd left. "I'll make sure you meet her before you move away. Or we can come out and visit you if it goes that far. She's nice. And she is beautiful. I don't know how she feels about me, because frankly, I'm afraid to ask her. She'll have no trouble pointing out my many flaws."

"Good for her. She isn't going to be a pushover to you." He laughed when Mary did, feeling better more and more about all this. "You remember what your mother told you, young man. Don't you dare use that thing for sex unless you know you can afford the consequences of your actions. Understand me?"

"I do. More than anyone. Yes, I'll be good." He hadn't thought of sex with Tabby, but now that it was mentioned, he could see them having a nice— "Mary, you're going to be ever so proud of me. All of you will."

"See that I am."

Whistling, he made his way to his room. There was little here that he couldn't live without. It had been nothing more than a place to sleep for a long time. But he was going to change that when he started over. He was going to maybe hire a decorator to make his house into a home if that was how it worked. Whatever he did, he was going to enjoy every moment that came his way.

~*~

Tabby caught herself thinking of Caleb again and shook off the thoughts as best she could. The damned man had only been around her for one day, and she was acting like a lovesick cow now. The laughter behind her had her turning toward it.

"Thinking of Caleb again, were you?" She asked Kylie how she knew. "Ah, so you are thinking of him. Good. He's a wonderful man. And he's got a good head on his shoulders. Unlike most of the men I date, he also has a job."

Tabby sat down in her chair. "I don't know what it is about him that has me thinking about him. A random thought will pop into my head, and I find myself thinking of what he'd think about it or something. Anyway, what do you have for me today?" She handed her the paperwork that had color-coded sticky tabs on them. "This is wonderful how you give them to me in order of importance for the day. I know you're not my secretary, but I do hope you train mine so that she's this efficient."

"No one would be nearly as efficient as my sister." They both turned to Arthur when he spoke. "Caleb will be coming by to see you this afternoon. He has some things he'd like to talk to you about on another matter. I don't know what it is, so don't pepper me with questions I'm not going to be able to answer."

"When has that ever stopped me before?" Kylie took the paperwork he had and put it on the bottom of the stack she already had in her hands. "You should know that as per requested, I've set up your 401k the way you wanted it. All the money you were paid for back pay is now in your checking account. If I were you, I'd think about putting more of it into retirement. That way, you aren't going to be in a larger tax bracket."

"All right." Arthur sat down when Kylie did. "I know you said you didn't know what Caleb was going to ask me, but do you know when he is returning? I'm just curious because Sheppard asks me every time I see him about the return. Like I'd have some sort of special knowledge."

She'd meant it as a joke, but it had failed miserably. Arthur seemed oblivious to her attempt, but Kylie laughed. Changing the subject again, she looked down at the paperwork in her hands and tried to read what was there. She was embarrassed.

"He said he was coming in later this afternoon. I've been looking for places for him to rent while he's here this time. It's going to be an extended stay so he can get to know Mr. and Mrs. Anderson." Kylie asked if he was looking for a home to buy or a rental. "I've been lining him up with not just houses, but a couple of sites that he can use for his work. And I wasn't told on rental or purchases. He just wanted a place of his own while here."

"That's nice, right? Getting to know his grandparents a little." Tabby nodded but was thinking of something that had popped into her head. "What? I know that look. You've thought of something else, haven't you? Like where he can live, perhaps?"

"No. Nothing like that. I was wondering if he'd be able to design the lunchroom. I know it's a small job, but the people I've contacted about a design want to charge nearly forty grand for them to just design the room. It's just going to be a breakroom for the people that work here, for cripes sake." Tabby knew it cost money to go to college, and having a degree was really expensive, and the contractors might need to recoup some of that money, but.... She shook her head as she continued. "I only wanted a room on each floor, so I could shove a bunch of vending machines in there so people could have a variety of things to eat and drink."

Arthur left them after a few minutes. Tabby had noticed that he and Kylie had lunch together every day. She wondered what they could have to talk about and realized it wasn't any of her business.

When Kylie left her as well, Tabby started working on her office. She'd not expected an office of such grandeur. Not only was it large, with all kinds of features she'd never had before, but it had a view. A beautiful view of the trees that started a deep forest behind the parking lot that belonged to this place. The parking lot was well maintained too, so it wasn't that much of a hardship to look out and enjoy the view.

Tabby stacked the water she'd brought in near the fridge. The sucker was as full as she could get it now. Her plan had been to load it with fresh snacks, but that went out the window when she realized how much work she had to do now that she was in charge. There wasn't any way she'd be able to run on just a few carrots and some dip. Smiling to herself, she was gathering up her trash just as her cell phone rang.

"I'm so glad I caught you in your office. Do me a favor, please. Can you look out your window and see my car? I'm standing next to it." She knew the voice but didn't want to be too obvious about how happy she was to hear from Caleb. Tabby told him she could see him. "Good. Come down and enjoy lunch with me. I have a couple of things I want to talk to you about. I have fresh subs from Mario's. I'm to understand they have a meatball sub that is out of this world."

"Kylie told you." Caleb laughed and told her to come and join him. "All right, but you'll have to help me put together two chairs that I got. When it said some assembly required, I didn't know that meant I had to practically build them. And I don't think anyone had any sort of knowledge of how few tools I have here. Or anywhere, for that matter."

"Usually, they send the tools you need

along with the order. But I will gladly come to your rescue. Are you coming down to enjoy this lovely day and have a meatball sub with me?" He cursed. "I forgot drinks. Do you happen to have any water there?"

"I do, as a matter of fact. I'll be down in a few minutes."

Grabbing four bottles of water after putting her phone in her back pocket, she made her way to the elevators. All of them were now working, she could see.

There were things going on in the building that she had ordered worked on. The elevator to the main floors had been out for some time now and was causing people to be at their job site anywhere from ten to twenty minutes late, depending on how many were in the queue to ride it.

She was in the bright sunlight in just a few minutes, and Caleb was there to greet her. He'd been talking to one of the employees who was also on the lot and seemed to be enjoying their conversation. When he took her hand into his, Tabby almost missed what he'd been saying to her.

"That was Mr. Carper. I think that's what

he said. He was telling me you're doing a bang-up job as the new plant supervisor, and he was glad someone was making sure you were eating. I didn't know what to think when he told me that you'd been working day and night on getting things in a better position." She handed Caleb the water bottles as he guided her to the woods. "I must confess, I've been trying my best to figure out a way to bring you out here to talk to you. I'm not shy by any means, but I am a little rusty when pursuing a woman."

She was still standing there when he turned and looked back at her. "You're pursuing me? I mean, this isn't a business lunch where you're going to tell me what I need to do and not do concerning your grandparents' business?"

"Okay, first of all, yes. I am pursuing you. I like you a great deal, and I'd like to take you out. Also, a great deal. As for telling you what to do here? I haven't any idea why you'd think I'd have any say in what you do. But the Andersons are only my grandparents because we share a bloodline that comes through to me. I know them less than I know what goes on behind the doors of that building." Caleb grinned at her as he came back to take her hand again. "Besides, I doubt very much that many people get by with telling you what to do when you have an idea in your head. You seem pretty headstrong. Not stupid, never that, but you know what needs to be done and have no issue in getting on it right away."

There was a table set up with cloth napkins and placemats. Along with the two chairs that looked much too comfy to be considered outdoor chairs, there was a large picnic basket and a bowl of what looked like fruit on the table. She looked at him when he helped her push her chair up to the table.

"You keep pursuing me like this, and you might get lucky." He nearly fell on his way to his chair. Coming back to her, he lifted her chin up and kissed her quickly on the mouth. "I'm sorry. Sometimes I don't think about what I'm saying until something outrageous comes flying out of my mouth."

"I love it." He poured their waters over the glasses of ice that were there. "Yes, by the way, Kylie told me you liked the subs there. I have to confess, I never enjoyed a meatball sub when I was a kid. Mom made meatballs one time, and they were a complete disaster. After that, she would buy a bag of them for us to have for pasta. Mom could cook when she had specific recipes. However, she was never any good at winging it, as Mary says."

"I enjoy the art of cooking—however, it's the cleanup I loathe. And usually, when I'm in the kitchen for more than microwaving some popcorn, which I burn nearly half the time, I have a huge mess going on." He asked her how she burned popcorn. "I get distracted. Not like I would zone out or anything, but I'd think of something that needed to be done, and instead of waiting until later to do it, I'd just wander off and start on it. It's why my apartment is in disarray right now. I'm cleaning out my closets and my pantry at the same time. The pantry was easier. All the things in it had expired years ago."

Enjoying her time with Caleb, they talked about themselves a great deal. Mostly it seemed that she was doing the talking, but Tabby did know a little more about him than she thought the people closest to him knew. He was still grieving hard for the loss of his mom, too.

"I've put my house on the market. It was a good home for Mom and myself, but I've decided I don't want to live there with the memories we had. It's not something I had to think hard on. Mary and Ben, my friends as well as staff, have decided they'd like to move out west. Ben has some health issues, and the weather would be better for him. I'll miss them a great deal. Will you have dinner with me tonight?" She stared at him with her mouth open. "You can say no, you know."

"I do know. And yes, I'd love to have dinner with you. Another round of subs?" Laughing, Caleb told her he could do better than that for her. "All right. I'd love that. I'm sort of rusty on dating myself just so you know. I do date, but it's mostly just blind dates, or one of my friends needs a second person there in the event things get wonky. Usually, they don't, but they're cautious."

"As everyone should be." Cleaning up the papers that they'd used, Caleb pulled some grapes off the bowl that they'd both been munching on since they'd finished the subs. "My mom set me up. Not with malice, I don't think, but having me come out here and meet her parents was her way of getting us together."

"Are you upset with that?" He shook his head and smiled. "Ah, so you like them. That's as good a start as anything, I guess. I didn't know them either. Shep rarely spoke about anything but himself. And that was usually his way of bragging about what things he'd been up to. He's not a bad person, I don't think. I've said that before. But I do think he'll come around. I have no idea why I think that. Perhaps I just want to believe it. I can see the two of you coming to terms over a great many things."

"I'd like that too. I have a meeting with him tomorrow morning. I just realized I'd like you to be there." She said she could do that as long as it was before ten. "Already working me into your schedule, are you?"

"No. I think I could easily clear an entire day to spend time with you." He reached for her hand, and she interlocked her fingers with his. "This is going to get out of hand quickly, isn't it, Caleb?"

"Out of hand? No. I think it's going just where we both want it to be." He leaned over and kissed the back of her hand. "Yes, I think this is going to be just fine for us."

Tabby hoped so. She really was liking this man. But she also knew it would only be until he found someone more like him. Sophisticated.

Wealthy. A beautiful doll-like person that would hang on his arm and worship him in ways Tabby didn't think she was capable of doing for anyone.

Chapter 4

House hunting wasn't going as easily as he had thought it would. As soon as he stepped into the third house in as many hours, he realized something. He was an architect. Laughing, he told the realtor he'd changed his mind.

"I'd like some land to build on. The more, the better." He told him he had plenty of land in this town that he could get cheaply. "Great. I want you to buy it all. I have plans of expanding some things around here."

"So, you're staying?" He looked at Arthur and told him he supposed he was. The man had been the perfect match for him over the last couple of days. "Good. I think the women will be happy to hear that. Kylie was telling me the other morning that she thought you were good for us. I have to admit, I love working with you. You're not at all what I imagined it would be like working for a wealthy man."

"Your grandda didn't tell you anything about me?" Arthur told him he'd said they'd have to form their own opinion but that he was a nice man. "I guess that's a good idea. He didn't tell me all that much about you two either, now that I think on it."

The realtor came back and said he had several pieces of property that could show Caleb. As they were headed out the door and to their cars, he thought of something else. Silly, he knew, but he wondered to himself what Tabby would think of his idea of the perfect house.

He and his mom would write down things they'd been asked to put into a home for someone. Things they had thought were a good idea and things they didn't think would work on any scale. The list had been very long when they'd started, the one about things that they wanted, but almost as soon as they saw the way it worked, whatever it was, they decided it wasn't for them. The most hilarious thing they'd thought every household would love was two sets of washers and dryers. It turned out that the two of them thought there should be one on every floor. Doing laundry was a pain in the butt when it had to be carried up and down the stairs all the time.

The first tract of land was near the little town. He didn't know what he'd do with it but thought it was too small to build much of any kind of business on. Purchasing it with the knowledge that he had to use it or lose it made him think the town was more desperate for businesses coming in than he'd first thought.

The second strip was much more in line with what he wanted.

"There is water and electric on this property that runs over to the next land for sale. There had been a house here as well as a large barn, but according to our records, lightning hit the house and took it and the barn out." He purchased both of those, too, glad for Arthur's input on some of the things he was to ask for in return for paying cash. "Mr. Anderson, there is a house with two hundred acres that just came on the market about two minutes ago. My boss told me to let you know."

"Let's go see it." It wasn't far, he was told, but just on the outskirts of town on the same end that the Andersons lived in. Tabby called him as they were headed there. "I'm looking at houses. What are you doing?"

"Not looking at houses. I have an apartment." He convinced her that she could meet him at the property he was headed to. "All right. But I have no opinion either way. And you still owe me for putting chairs together."

"I'll get to that too." He was laughing when he pulled up in front of the house. "I'm waiting for you to see this. I think you might be willing to live in a house when you see this one."

As soon as she got there and stood outside her car, Caleb watched her face. She was as excited to see the inside as he was. It took him a moment or two to realize that the realtor, he thought his name was Cain, was telling them the history of the house.

"Mrs. Bundy died last night in a nursing home. The family, her husband's, wants to take the house and live there as a group. There are provisions for this not to happen in the laws of the county, I'm to understand. Since she was in the nursing home for just a little over a decade, the family, both sides, I guess, haven't paid the taxes or any of the utilities since they expected the money to come from the estate. There was none." Tabby asked why the power was on. "That too was supposed to have been paid. However, no one did. The city left it on hoping that when anyone moved into the house, they'd not have the expense of having to replace pipes and such when it froze up."

Caleb was handed a long list of information, which he simply handed to Arthur. As soon as he walked up the wide long steps to the wraparound porch, he knew he was going to make this work. Tabby took his hand into hers, squeezing tightly as the door was opened for them. Arthur read off what had been sent to Cain.

"Furnace and air conditioner are eleven years old. It seems to work well, it says here. I'd still replace it. The furniture has been well maintained. Once a month, the bank sends someone over to check for mice and other creatures when the lawn is taken care of." They were entering what he could only assume was the library. "There are books that belong on the shelves. They've been put into storage nearby to keep them from being harmed. It says here it's 'as is.' What are they talking about, Cain?"

Nodding, he put his phone away before

answering him. "As in the furniture that is here goes with the house. They don't believe they'll be able to sell it for any profit anyway. There are some things in storage, as you've heard. I'm not entirely sure what that might entail, but I'll find out. The bank is talking to my boss right now about a price they'll need to cover the expenditures that have been accrued with the house since Mrs. Bundy was put into the nursing home." Arthur asked about the family. "The will is to be read in a few days. As far back as anyone can remember, Mrs. Bundy didn't care all that much for either side of the family. She had no children with Mr. Bundy, and the house was hers before they wed. I believe this might be the first case of a prenup I've ever heard of."

They walked through the living room and to the dining room. The room needed work—the window in the big window had been broken and then boarded up. But it hadn't been able to keep the rain from coming in, so there was some damage. This time it was Tabby that was taking notes.

The house was in good shape, considering that no one had been in it for a decade. He noticed the way Tabby eyed the furniture, the way she seemed to be checking for mouse droppings. He admired the fact that she was showing how unimpressed she was with the place. However, every time she held his hand, the way she was trembling told him that her desire for the place was huge. There was very little needed to convince him to buy it — even less when he got to factor in that the house was Tabby's dream too.

"Are you a good negotiator?" He told Arthur he wasn't too bad at it. "Good. I suck. I can do it in a courtroom, but when something is for sale, like at a garage sale or an auction, I just pay what is asked of me. I don't do value in furniture or homes well."

"I'll do it." Tabby looked at him when he laughed. "You don't think I could get the best price for us? I mean you?"

"I think you can do whatever you set your mind to. I think I've said this to you before."

She nodded.

When Cain found them in the kitchen, he sat down at the country table that had seen better days and laid his head on the table before Caleb sat across from him when Tabby did. "Bad news?"

"Depends on how you look at it, I guess.

Mr. Shimer at the bank and Mr. Douglas, my boss, said they've worked out a deal that will make everyone happy. Not including you. You, they said, are just a pain in their ass right now. I haven't any idea. But since you've been really honest with me and have given me this chance to work with you, I'm going to be straight up with you, Mr. Anderson." Caleb nodded, unsure where this man was going. "I need a job, and I have a feeling that when you put your head to something, you get it done. Like what you said earlier about buying up the land to make more business for the town. Anyway. I'm really great at this job. I know that, as does Mr. Douglas. That's the only reason he keeps me around, I think. That way, he can take half of what I should make in commissions as well as his cut."

"Did he say something to you that has you telling me this?" Cain said it was water under the bridge. "Not as far as I'm concerned it's not. What did he tell you? Or threaten you with."

"I'm probably going to be fired anyway after this. But if you want the house, I'd not pay any more than about five grand for it. You could, I suppose, but that's the total cost needed to care for the bills from here." Tabby asked him what they wanted him to pitch to them. "Fifty grand. There is a lot of land here, as I said to you before. Enough that you could do just about anything you wish, and no one would know. The other parcels of land that you've told me you were going to purchase were earmarked, not my idea, for the bank to use for prospective buyers from out of town."

"You were told that you were to tell me I can't buy them. That someone else has, weren't you?" Cain nodded. "I see. Arthur, can you take care of this for me? And see to it that any other plots of land around and near here are purchased as well. I'd like it to be filed now if there is a way for you to do it."

"I will have to contact some people out of town to make it work for us." Tabby said that would be fine, and Arthur walked away, already pulling out his cell phone. They both looked at Cain when he thanked them. Arthur turned back. "The house too?"

"Yes." Both he and Tabby answered at the same time. She smiled at him and called him a jerk — why he had no idea. "For bringing me here so that I'd have to move in with you. I know we've not had a date yet, but I want to live here with all that I am, and if I have to put up with your ugly mug to do so, then I guess I will." She turned to Cain. "I have six job openings at the place I'm running right now. Any one of them I think you would be suited for. Also, the pay is good, and I can offer you benefits right up front."

"I'll take it." Cain shook both their hands. "The property at the end of this land is for sale as well. I'm sure Arthur will find it. It's another five hundred acres that also has been earmarked." Nodding, he called his attorney back, and he had indeed found it. "I have a wife and a new baby on the way. Working for her dad, Mr. Douglas, isn't anything I ever wanted to do. But I was one of the hundreds cut from working at the grocery store warehouse a few months back. I'll be honest with the two of you again here. My wife and I are being treated like indigents by Mr. Douglas. That's what I was told to call him. He comes into the house whenever he wants. Somehow he has a key, and every time I change the locks, he just gets another one. I finally gave up on that. A cleaning service comes by the house the day he's coming for dinner, which lately is nightly. Nothing we ever do is right or safe for his grandson. We're having a girl, and he simply refuses to believe it. Lily, my wife, is afraid that when she has our daughter, her dad will bully or pay someone off to make sure we come home with a son rather than what we have."

"Does he pay for your house? Rent or something like that?" Caleb wanted to know that as well and was happy that Tabby had asked. Cain said Mr. Douglas owned the house, and they were required to pay rent. "Well, that's not right." She turned to him. "I don't suppose you know of a place he can live until we get this fixed, do you?"

"I have the perfect place for them." Cain said he couldn't do that. "Yes, you can. My mom and I were given the same sort of help when I was about five. Without the help, there is no telling how we might have gotten where we are today. I'll make a call right now, and we'll have you moved in— Are any of the things in the house anything you want?"

"No. A few items that will fit in a suitcase. Pictures, but nothing we purchased." He laughed a little. "I don't know what to say about this. I mean, you have no idea how much this is going to mean to us and our growing family."

Caleb did know. And he wasn't kidding

about them getting a hand up. It had been Mary and Ben that had helped them by cosigning on the house they'd lived in up until his mother had passed away. Talking to Arthur while Cain called his wife, he told him to buy the two houses he'd seen earlier today. Nodding that he would, he made his way to the room he thought would be the study.

After deciding he was as much in love with this room as he was all the others, he turned to Tabby when she entered the room. She looked beautiful with the sunlight from the stained glass window behind him. The desk that had also been left behind was the perfect place for him to sit while he thought about all the things he wanted to do to her.

"Cain is going to start working next week. I hope you don't mind, but I have Kylie looking into some things he mentioned after you left. Do you have him a home?" He nodded and said that it would need to be furnished. "Can I move in here with you? If so, he can have what I have at my apartment to start off with. And anything you might have left over at your home."

"I spoke to Mary this morning before heading out. They've taken very little, so there would be plenty more for him to round out the edges of the house. It's five bedrooms, so he can grow as much as he needs to. And I would be happier than I think I've ever been if you were to move in here with me." She moved around the desk to the window that looked out over the expanse of their backyard. "What is it you're thinking about, Tabby? Something that I can do or help you with?"

She turned to look at him, and he could see the tears as they made their way down her cheeks. Moving towards her, he held her in his arms while she spoke in broken random sentences that he didn't really understand until she asked him not to break her heart.

Tabby made her way back to work with a lighter heart. She was still afraid that Caleb was going to hurt her, but what he'd told her had reassured her that he was going to try his best not to hurt her in any way. She really felt foolish for sobbing like she had, but it had been weighing heavily on her mind and heart, especially after being glib about her moving in and him taking her so seriously. The conversation the two of them had had would be with her forever, she thought. And it had only been his declaration of making sure she was happy that made her feel like he was falling into this relationship as quickly and as head over heels in love as she was. Only the man in the parking lot when she pulled in, Shep, made her feel the sinking heart feeling all over again.

"I just want to talk to you. Please?" Nodding, she told him security was going to be aware that he was in the building with her. "I deserve that. All right. I'm going to be on my best behavior. I promise you. I've gone to see my parents today. We had an exceptionally long talk."

"Good for you. I'm hoping you're not here to take my job from me. I will fight you for it." Shep laughed. "I don't think this is funny, Shep. I've been working extremely hard here since I was put in charge."

He whistled when they entered the building. "You have been. Christ, this is amazing." She realized she had forgotten to ask Caleb for help with the break rooms when Shep entered the one that was currently being used. "I love how you've had the concrete taken down to let in the sunshine. It makes the room seem larger and brighter."

Showing him around made her feel better. He was complimenting her on the things that she'd done already and suggesting things she'd not thought of. Making her way to her new office, she laughed a little when she found not just Arthur putting her chairs together, but Cain was working on them as well. There was a message on her desk for her to call the contractor.

"I have to do this. Will you wait?" Just as he said he'd come back, Kylie joined them. She said she'd take him around to see the rest of the things that were going on. "Are you sure you don't mind? I won't be long, I don't think."

"Take your time. We'll work around the building, and I can point out things that you have going on. Besides, I think you have some paperwork to sign off on with Caleb. Arthur said he has things squared away for you guys." She glanced at Arthur, and he winked at her. "I'll be fine."

~*~

Shep hadn't been so impressed in all his life. In just a few short days, not only were things moving to improve the areas that people worked in, but he could see that the employees seemed to be having a good time. Of course, he'd not spent a great deal of time here, much less on the floor, but he liked what he was seeing.

Finally, they ended up in the room that was earmarked for a break room. There was nothing to show for it, not yet, but someone had put up sticky notes—he thought it might have been Kylie—as to where things were going to go.

"I had a long talk with my parents." She asked him how that had gone. "That wasn't what changed my mind about myself. I am a jerk. But since my dad didn't know I was coming, he wasn't there. A doctor's appointment that he'd made weeks ago. Anyway, my plan had been to be there to talk him into letting me come home and not have to work. But then I wandered in the dining room and found all these photo albums."

"Abby's." He nodded. "Caleb brought them at the request of your parents. They wanted to see her, as they had missed so much of her life."

"I didn't know people did that anymore. Made those silly albums with stickers and stuff all around them. But I could see her doing it. Anyway, I started looking through the one that was open. She and Caleb had been on some kind of cruise. It wasn't until I realized how I was looking at pictures of my sister that it hit me that she was gone." Kylie told him she was sorry. "So am I, to be honest with you. After I had myself a long cry, which I won't admit to anyone else, I put the albums in order and looked at each page, trying to imagine what she'd had to go through to get to the point where she was by the time she'd been on the cruise with Caleb."

Shep thought about some of the pictures he'd seen. "The first album had a great many pictures of her and her belly growing. Ultrasound pictures of Caleb's growth. For a tiny little thing, she was huge with her son." Kylie warned him not to say that to any other woman. "I won't. I'm not *that* stupid. But I could see that despite living where she was — it looked like a women's shelter — she was doing well. Happy too."

"Caleb said she rarely got down. When she was at the end of her life, she wasn't as strong, of course, but she didn't let it take her under too far. Caleb said they would talk for as long as she could stay awake those last few days, then he'd go and work. I think he's still hurting for his loss." Shep didn't feel he had the right to say he was hurting too. He had pushed her away as much as his parents had. "It's all right if you're hurting for her, Shep. I'm sure she would have felt for you if things had been swapped."

"She was a bigger person than I was. Even as children." He had thought of her as a teenager a great deal in the last twenty-four hours. "Abby was older than me by about ten years. I was almost seven when she left home. Even back then, I was a shit. But after she left, my parents — not blaming them — but they sort of became ghosts of what they had been before. I know now that I was trying to get their attention by acting out. It worked, but not the way I had hoped. After a while, I just made a habit of being a prick. To everyone. Since they never took any notice of what I was doing to get back at them, I got worse and worse. Until my own nephew knocked me down a couple of times."

"Yes, well, he is a good deal younger than you are. And stronger. In better shape too. I'm betting that he —" He laughed, telling her he got it. "Someone should have knocked you around long before now, I'm thinking."

"And I'd agree with you. Now, I mean." He looked around the room. "I was a shit to Tabby. And when I showed up today, I knew for sure she was going to call the police on me. But she was nice and polite to me. Even showing me around the place like I was a prospective employee."

"You could be." Shep looked at her, trying hard not to get his hopes up. To work here, beside Tabby instead of against her, was what he'd been thinking about. He'd not even talked to his dad about it when he returned from the doctor. "I have to hire sixteen more people before the renovations are done. Also, Tabby is adding more projects that will be umbrellaed under the same name. Things that will not just help the community in hiring more people, but they'll also be trained on things such as computers and things like that. You could help with that. In fact, Shep, you could do whatever you like. You're far from stupid. Construction jobs are open as well."

"I really would like to do that. Work with construction." She nodded and stood up from the cable roll they had been sitting on. "Right now? You're going to hire me right now?"

"I don't see any reason why not. There are two construction crews working right now that need a man. It's nothing more than a labor job, but it pays well, and you could use the exercise before I put you out to work." He stood up, his heart pounding so hard he was sure she could hear it. "You seem to be dressed well enough for the job. I'm glad. But I will warn you, Shep. You cause any shit while working here, and you won't have to worry about Caleb knocking the shit out of you. I will hurt you in ways that will make you remember me for the rest of your numbered days."

"Will you have dinner with me?" He closed his mouth and covered it with his hand. "I'm so sorry. I have no idea where that came from."

"Yes. I'd like to have dinner with you." Shep asked her if she was serious. "If you were, I am. I like you, Shep. A lot. But I'm not kidding you when I tell you that I won't put up with any of your shit."

"No. I'm not going to promise you I'll be on my best behavior all the time. I might slip back, but I'm sure you'll have no trouble at all making me come around." She doubled up her fist, and he pulled it to his mouth and kissed it before he could change his mind. "If you're ready, we can go now. I haven't any idea where we'll go, but even if we end up with fast food, I'll be happy just to be spending time with you."

He found that he was excited too. Taking her hand when she let him, Shep felt like he could have taken on the world at that moment and — well, he wasn't foolish enough to think that he'd come out anywhere but on the bottom part of the pile, but he was feeling like a new man.

They ended up at her hotel. The dining room was open, and that was where they ate. He was so happy it took him until the check came to realize he had no money. Not even a credit card. Laughing, as if she knew, she put her credit card on the tray, and it was whisked away.

"I know your situation, Shep. Besides, I have a company card that I'm to use. I think this is the first time I've used it, and I couldn't have asked for a better partner to do that with." He told her he was sorry. "Don't be. The next time you can pay. There will be a second time, right?"

"Yes. I hope so." They were leaving the restaurant when they saw Tabby and Caleb. "They're a nice couple. I mean, they are a couple, right?"

"They are. I think they sort of complete each other. The other day when they came back from looking around, I think Tabby was walking about a foot off the ground. She tries hard not to go all googly when he's around, though." Shep laughed and was happy for his nephew. "The two of them will be a very powerful couple too, I'm thinking. The world will be set on its ear when they start something."

He watched them until they noticed the two of them. Neither of them made fun of him for being with Kylie, for which he was grateful. When they invited them to join them for an ice cream across the street, it was Kylie that said yes, and they made their way there.

Shep was sure someone was going to comment on the two of them. It had been a date, he thought. However, he didn't want to read too much into it. Kylie didn't seem to care what anyone thought and told them what a wonderful date they'd had.

"Shep, you're going to have to get over your insecurities." His face heated up when Tabby spoke. "I'm glad the two of you are getting together. I can't think of a better couple than the two of you."

"I'm older than her." Kylie laughed and told him she liked older, mature men. "I'm not sure how mature I am, but I think I'm about fifteen years older than you."

"No. you're older, but not nearly that much. You're somewhere around thirty-five, right?" He told her that he'd be thirty-six on his next birthday. "I'm almost afraid to ask you, but how old do you think I am? A hint to you is that I'm older than my brother by a few years."

"I thought you were in your early twenties or something." No one laughed at him, and it was Kylie that smiled. "You're older than that, aren't you?"

"Yes. I'll be thirty-one on my next birthday. I went to law school after my grandma passed away. Mostly it was to have something to do with my grandfather. Then when Arthur decided to join his firm, I finished up just about the time my brother did. We have been partners for a while now too." She smiled at him again. "So you see, we're not that different, the two of us. Two people that have had a late start on life in general, and now we've met each other. Where will it go? Who knows. But for now, I'm happy as I've been for a while."

"So am I." He was very happy and enjoyed his ice cream cone. "I don't remember the last time I had a cone, much less one that I ate like this. Out in the open."

"You need to get out more. Socialize. Get to know the people you're going to be working with." Kylie told Caleb and Tabby that he was going to be working with the construction crew. And once again, he was surprised by their acceptance. "I'll help you with the socializing. You'll see, we'll know everyone by the end of the month."

Shep had spent his entire life in this town, and he'd bet that he couldn't count ten people that he knew. Less than that whose names he knew. Yes, he thought, this was going to be a good deal of fun. So long as he didn't fuck up, he told himself. And he was going to try his best not to do that.

Chapter 5

Caleb was looking over the paperwork on his land purchases when someone started pounding on the door. Calling for Arthur after looking in the security camera, the two of them went to the door and opened it.

"May I help you?" The man tried to barge his way in, but Caleb wasn't having any of it. "If you want to come in here, you're going to have to explain to me why you tried your best to break down my front door. I just bought this house, and I'd like to be able to live here for a while before—"

"Where do you get off buying this house? Or, for that matter, all the damned land around town? I'm in charge of that shit, and you'll just have them take your name off the paperwork right fucking now. Or else." Caleb looked at his watch and told the realtor that it was a little early in the morning to be making threats. "Are you serious? I don't threaten people, kid. I make promises, and I'm going to make you turn over that property to me right now, or I'm going to take you to court. See if I don't."

"You won't." The man, Dick Douglas—a more ridiculous name than he'd ever heard—asked him what he was talking about. "You. You said you were going to take me to court, and that isn't going to happen. What I did was purchase land for the asking price that was for sale by your company. I didn't even haggle, even though I think I could have gotten them much cheaper than they were priced. However, I think that had more to do with you wanting to purchase them at a lower price than me getting a good deal. All the paperwork has been filed. Legally, I might add. And my name is filed on all the deeds now. I would have thought that your buddy, Slam-dunk, would have told you about it. I must ask, why do they call him that? Slam-dunk implies that he might well have played basketball, but I think he's much too short—"

"What the hell are you going on about?

Christ. Quit emptying your head and tell me when you're going to do as I want." Caleb said again that he wasn't going to do any such thing. "You don't know what you're doing, kid."

"Caleb Anderson." He looked confused again. "My name. Instead of kid, I thought you'd call me by my name." The man looked like his head was going to explode. That encouraged Caleb to be more creative in pissing the man off. "Of course, you could continue to call me kid if you're in the mood. It's doubtful that anyone else would think of me as a child. But you go right on ahead and—"

The gun came out of the back of the man's pants. When it was pointed at him, Caleb didn't move. Nor did he allow his fear to show through. Arthur said he'd call the police just as Tabby pulled into the drive. She was out of her car and up on the porch before either man could warn her to stop and stay back.

"What the hell is going on here? Why do you have a gun pointed at him?" Dick told her to mind her own business. "Do you think it sounds like I'm going to do that? Mind my own business? I'm not, in the event your head couldn't handle thinking and standing at the same time. How the hell do you even make sure you're bringing air in and out when—? Never mind. You made this my business when you pointed a gun at the chest of the man I love."

"You love me?" She grinned and nodded. "I love you too. I know this is quick and all, but will you marry me? Make me even happier than I am—"

"I'm fucking standing right here. With a gun." Tabby told Dick to hush. "You people are certifiable. I'm going to have to kill one of you in order for you to pay me any mind, aren't I?"

"The police are on their way. And congratulations, Tabby and Caleb. Love must be in the air."

Dick started cursing, then acted like there wasn't a thing wrong when the first cruiser pulled into their driveway. He still had his gun pointed at Caleb, and he thought for sure the man was going to blow his nuts off when the officer put his own hand on Dick's gun and told him to drop it.

"There is just a small misunderstanding here, Officer." He was told again to drop the gun. Caleb made his way out onto the porch, and in front of Tabby, in the event the idiot managed to get himself killed. "I was just asking the kid here—Caleb—what kind of interest he was getting on the property loans he took out this week."

"Mr. Douglas was threatening me with his gun about how I was to void my deeds on the properties I purchased this morning. Apparently, he thought he should have been the one that purchased it." The officer told Dick once more to drop the gun. He finally did, and Caleb was relieved that no one was hurt. "I'd like to press charges, Office Kimble. If you could please take him away from here, I can have my attorney or myself come down to the station house and take care of this right away."

"Your attorney is fine to come down, Mr. Anderson. I heard someone bought the property out here. Couldn't ask for better neighbors." Tabby asked him where he lived. "About two miles down this road. My dad used to work the farm here when it was still viable. Many people came out here in the fall to gather up pumpkins and in the spring again to get some strawberries. If you need someone to show you where those patches are, I can send my son down. Billy has been biting his lip to come and see if you're going to have horses to ride again."

Caleb didn't have to look at Tabby to know she was excited. After Dick was put in the cruiser, Sherman Kimble called his son and had him come down. Even from a few feet away, Caleb could hear the boy's excitement. As soon as the cruiser pulled out of the drive, a tractor that had to be older than the house they lived in came rumbling down the road.

"My name is Billy Kimble. My dad said you might need some help around here." Tabby told him what they were looking for. "Sure, I can show you where they are. Mom and I used to come here every fall when I was little. Most of the time in the spring, too, when the berries would come on. I used to eat my weight in them, Mrs. Bundy told me once when we went to visit her in the nursing home. Nice lady too. Her kids aren't, but she sure was. How do you want to do this?"

"When we first moved out here, we purchased a golf cart to ride around in. Do you think you could drive us around in that?" Caleb thought that if anyone put a wire on this kid, they could have powered the country. "All right. I'm going to take that as a yes. Just give me a second to make sure my friend knows where we're going."

Caleb started for the house again, then stopped. Going back, he kissed Tabby on the mouth and turned back. He could get used to this, he thought. Having someone around that had his back all the time. After telling Arthur where they were going, he handed him his working pad and told him to take pictures, that it was set up to show the exact location.

"This will be a good opportunity for you to find out where you wish to put the barn, as well as the other outbuildings you were talking about." Nodding, he wondered how long the kid could stay here and help them. "I'd hire him. Even if he only rode around the area and showed you things, it would be well worth your time to have him working for you. Not to mention, if you do decide to do the pumpkins this year or ever, he'd be the one that could get it started for you."

Billy turned out to be a wonderful source of information. Not just on where the gardens had been, but that in the fall, Mrs. Bundy would have a sort of round-up for the kids. It was attended by nearly every county surrounding them.

"Dad told me it was just a social event. There would be some people selling their wears and some of their late garden things. There would even be shucking contests, as well as a roasting hog." Tabby peppered Billy with questions as they drove through what had been the strawberry patch. "My goodness, Ms. Tabby. I'm betting come spring, if you got someone out here now to fix this up, you'd have enough strawberries to have a picking party."

It wasn't as overgrown with weeds as Caleb thought it would have been. But there were rows and rows of the strawberry plants just sunning themselves in the morning sun. He estimated the rows to be about two hundred feet long, and there were six rows. Tabby asked Billy what happened to the berries that wouldn't be picked.

"I don't know, but I can ask my dad. Mrs. Bundy had some jellies in her cupboard when my dad was there right after she died. I'm sure it's still there if you haven't tossed it out. She kept it in the basement. Kept it cooler, Dad told me." They were going to look when they got back. "What else did you want to see? The pumpkins are a nice treat. If you don't mind, I'll take in a wagon load of them to sell. Tell me how to price them."

"Why don't you have someone come out and help you gather them up, and you and he give them away? I'll pay you guys for your time." He thanked him but declined. "I have to insist, Billy. You've already been a great help to us, and I'd like to pay you so you'll be willing to come and help again. Besides, a nice kid like you needs some spending money for a date or two, right?"

"I don't date all that much. I like girls and all, but I'm really shy around them." He took the twenty that Caleb handed him. "I'll do you right, Mr. Anderson. I swear it."

"I don't have any trouble believing that at all, son." The barn, or what was left of it, wasn't worth trying to save. The slate, Billy told him, was worth some money to anyone doing crafty things. And he might well be able to sell off some of the barn wood there. "I will have to have your help on that as well. Helping me figure that sort of thing out."

Caleb took pictures of everything he thought might help with mapping out the land. The map that was in the courthouse was nice, but he'd bet anything that the land had changed enough around the house that there was little to resemble what he and Tabby had now.

By the time they'd gone over as much as they could on a full tank, they invited Billy to have lunch with them. He declined, saying he wanted to talk to his dad about coming out and picking the pumpkins out of the field before it got too late for plans to get them.

"The next time I take you around, you guys ride the cart, and I'll take a wagon on the back of the tractor. There are still some things growing out there wild, but I'm betting someone in town can make a meal or two out of them." He got up on the tractor but looked like he had something else to say. When he did, Caleb was impressed. "Mr. Caleb, there are a lot of people around that don't have two pennies to rub together without one of them squeaking a bit. If you don't mind one bit, I'll have my granny round up some of those women that she sews with and have them bring out some families that could use the stuff we found. Those potatoes might not be worth spit, but they're better than nothing at all."

"You're right." Tabby looked at Caleb and asked if he had money. After telling her they had plenty for whatever she was thinking, she said, "Billy, I want you to come by here tomorrow with your grannie, and we'll figure out something for these hungry people. Okay?"

"Sure. I can do that. Thank you so much for today. I sure did have fun."

After he left them, his tractor tossing up dust like it was plowing, they sat on the front porch. They were still sitting there when the cruiser went by their house. Billy and his dad were going to have a very eventful lunch, Caleb thought.

"What did you have in mind for the hungry people?" She told him the plan that had occurred to her at work and how she wanted to execute it. "Are you thinking of not using the business now as a soup kitchen?"

"I was wondering if you owned anything that might be a barn or thereabouts. Like a building we can use that would pass inspection. I don't want to get caught unawares with anything bad happening when we open the doors for this." He said there were two large buildings in the downtown area that would work. "One of them is the restaurant, you mean."

"Yes. I don't know how cleaned up it

is, but we can have a— We should talk about something first. It's not important, but it might go a long way in making sure you understand that the money is there for whatever you need. We're getting to that serious point, to the point where I'm looking forward to you marrying me. I know it's very quick, us getting married, and that we've not even kissed all that much— something I'd like to remedy as soon as we can. Dating has been a nightmare with everything else going on. But I have fallen in love with you and want to spend the rest of my life with you. If you do love me." She said she really did love him. "And I love you too. Okay, so here is the scoop, as my mom used to say. Can you tell me again that you love me as much as I do you?"

"Oh, so very much. And yes, I really would like to be your wife. I know you have some money, more than likely a great deal of it, so I'll sign a prenup if you wish." He told her he never wanted that. "I will. I would gladly do that. I love you that much."

"Good. Now, we have, as of the moment we get to the bank and sign paperwork, well over a hundred billion dollars. It's mostly in investments. A great deal of stocks and property.

We own three condo high-rises along some coasts that bring in a great deal of money all year round."

She put her hand over his mouth. "You said billion. A hundred billion dollars." He nodded. "I'm sure you meant that as a joke, right?"

He kissed her hand before removing it from his mouth. "I didn't want to overwhelm you too much." She laughed. "It really is closer to two hundred billion when you factor in the stocks and other items we have invested in. Tabby, we own grocery stores, car dealerships. There are entire malls that we own. Restaurants enough so that we could eat at one of them a day and never hit them all."

She put her hand over his mouth again. "You're seriously telling me that if I were to be your wife right now, I'd be a billionaire several times over. And that you'd not want me to sign anything to say I wouldn't get shit if I were to leave you." He asked her if she was going to leave him. "Never. But that's not the point. Caleb, you've worked extremely hard for this money."

"I have. So did my mom. But here's the thing, Tabby. I feel like I've been waiting my entire life for you to come along so I'd have someone to show the world to again. My mom and I went on these fabulous trips, sailed oceans and seas. Went to caves and mountain tops. Now, because I consider myself to be the luckiest man in the world, I get to do those same things with you at my side. I love you."

~*~

The building was perfect. Not only could they move the tables around so they could be more efficient, but they would also have enough room to set up the area in the back for storage for a pantry. Tabby was just figuring out the space that would be needed for the boxes she thought would be good for carrying things home once the place was filled when Sheppard cleared his throat.

"Do you know just about how big a ten-pound bag of potatoes might be? Like how much space they would take up." He said he could call the kitchen at home and ask. "Great. I have to make this work for potatoes that we'll order."

He told her the size of the bag after a few minutes. "Are you actually going to buy them in ten-pound bags? Why not buy them by the container—I believe they're called a lug or something like that—and bring them in bulk?

That way, since I'm assuming you're going to be giving them away, people can take as many or as few as they need." She kissed him on the cheek before she could change her mind about it. "I would like to speak to you about your work at the Anderson building."

"If you're upset about the cafeteria, then I'll pay for the difference. I talked to Caleb about it, and he said it would be more practical as well as employee-friendly to put in that rather than vending machines." He said he thought that was a great idea. "Then it's the part-time workers, isn't it? I wasn't sure I could make it work for the workers. But I think with the way they're working, we'll get more production out of them and—"

"Tabby." She closed her mouth and grinned at him. "I'm very pleased with what you have going on. All of it. I just wanted to get your opinion on having Shep work there. And to make sure you didn't hire him because you thought that was what I wanted."

"I wouldn't do that." She thought of something. "Come with me. I want to show you something. And if you tell anyone but your wife, I think it would upset him."

Taking him to the room that was going to have monitors set up for the security team that was going to be on duty at all times, she pulled up the camera where Shep was working. Just as he'd been when she's looked on him earlier, he was in the same room.

"They showed him what they wanted in the way of tile. Mr. Carson — he's in charge of the tile being laid — taught Shep the ins and outs of the job in about ten minutes. Once he got the flow and ebb of the job, Shep has laid two floors of tile in the last two days. They're not small rooms either, but large ones like offices." Another man joined Shep, and they spoke for several minutes. To see the other man laughing, not taking swipes at people, had done her heart some good. As soon as the other man left, Shep got right back to work. "He's made himself a name for getting the job done too. And at lunchtime, he and the others sit around talking and enjoying their time together like they've worked with him forever. He's doing a great job and seems to have a knack for construction."

Sheppard was still standing there looking at the monitor when she was called away. After joining her in the storage room, she could tell he'd been crying. Tabby asked him if he was all right.

"I am. Better than I think I have been for some time. I called my wife and showed her how he was working. She and I had a nice cry over it, happy tears that he seems to be fitting in finally." She asked him if he knew about him dating. "Kylie. I haven't seen them together, but he told us about it the other night at dinner. He's been staying at the house until he can get himself a place. I started to ask if I could help him out, and he flat out told me he's old enough that he needs to have been up on his feet for a while now. I'm very proud of him. But this, seeing him here today — well, I can't thank you enough for that."

"I didn't do it. He did this on his own. Shep told Kylie that he saw the photo albums on your dining room table the other day and had seen his sister's life. Something about him not having one. Not on his own nor with you and your wife. He blames himself for that too." Sheppard asked her what she was doing, changing the subject so he could gather up his emotions. "We've, as you might have guessed, bought a place in order to have a soup kitchen in it. Also, a sort of food pantry for those that need a boost-up. These shelves that we use here for storage are the same size as the ones I was thinking about getting for the pantry. I was just measuring to see how much I could put on them. Thanks for the idea on bulk. I didn't think of that."

"This restaurant you're using, do you know how many days a week you're going to open it? I'd like to help out if you don't mind. I know this is your project and—" She corrected him. "All right. I know this is a community project, so I don't want to step on any toes to make it work for the town."

"Hello, Mr. Anderson." He turned to see the elder Mrs. Kimble standing behind him. "The little miss there hired me to get my old bones up and working the kitchen she's putting in. Also, we're going to be dragging out some of them old men and women at the nursing home and dusting them off a bit to work as well. Might do the old ones a bit of good to have something to look forward to."

"My goodness, what a grand idea." Sheppard, as he asked her to call him, went on for several minutes on the idea of the nursing home. "I'm assuming it wouldn't be too difficult of a job for anyone. I don't want anyone hurting."

"Their doctor has to approve what they can do according to the list of things we might have them working with. And they get to enjoy a hot meal that ain't coming from a can too." She handed him a long sheet of paper that she and the elderly woman had gone over this morning. "We're not going to use instant if we can help it. Taters that we have to peel will be better for them. Also, in-season fruit will help with constitutions. Your son, he knew of a man that has himself some seconds in the way of grocery fruits and stuff that we're going to be taking off his hands. You should be proud of him for that bit of news, mister. He sure did save that food place a good deal of money."

"I am. As a matter of fact, I'm proud of all of you. Including you, Mrs. Kimble. I'm glad to see you didn't need much in the way of dusting off. You look as fit as you've always been." She thanked him, her face pinking up just a little. "I'd like to help with the project if you'd not mind. I'm betting that Melissa will get on board with it as well. She was just telling me the other day that she's kind of getting bored sitting around the house."

Tabby was still talking to the two of them

about working out a schedule when Caleb showed up to take her to lunch. In the end, Sheppard called Melissa, and she joined them as well. This afternoon they were going to move Cain and his family to their new place. Caleb's furniture had arrived last night.

Cain and his wife Elly went through the house and helped pick out what went into each room. There had been a great deal of furniture on the two moving trucks, and the two of them were happy with the washer and dryer, which they'd not been able to have before, as well as linens and all the nice things that had been brought. They were completely set up by two in the morning. But it was when Dick Douglas showed up that things got a little scary.

"What's going on here? Shouldn't you be out looking for a job, Cain? I'm sure if you get those deals back for me and take a cut in pay that I'll take you back." Cain told him he was working. "At what? A furniture salesman? Get up off your ass, boy, and get back to work first thing in the morning. However, you'll be working the office from now on. There won't be any more commission checks coming your way, so I'll have to take care that you have a roof over my daughter's head. That'll cost you."

"He told you he has a job." Tabby stepped up to the older bully and asked him what he was doing there. "I'm reasonably sure you know that Caleb owns this place, along with a great many others. Shouldn't you be in jail? Or did you have to have your little buddy, the banker come and bail you out? Why don't you go home and behave yourself before you end up back in jail."

Elly came out of the house then with several empty boxes. Caleb had gone to help her, and Dick laughed. "Looks to me like my daughter has finally come to her senses about you, Cain. She's found herself a real man." No one said anything, but it was Tabby that started laughing first. "You jealous? I have news for you, that man ain't worth spit. Neither of them are."

"You think so? Well, not that it matters, but Caleb asked me to marry him. He's being a polite person and helping your daughter." She looked between Elly and her dad. "She must take after her mother. Thankfully. She's nothing at all like you are. I think her kids are going to be wonderful too. Like I've told you before, go home. I'm not in the mood to fuck with you today."

He left them there, laughing all the way to his car. The fucker was going to get his comeuppance even if she had to dish it out herself. But tonight, Cain and Elly Longshore were going to be home in their own bed.

Cain said that Dick had come by their home earlier that morning and had demanded a raise in their rent, knowing full well that he'd lost his job. Tabby had an idea that she was using Cain all wrong. She needed to think on it a little, but she thought that Cain and his wife should be realtors. That would certainly put a pinch in the older man's ass. The more she thought about it, the more she loved the idea.

Of course, she was going to have to talk to Caleb about it, but the idea had merit. She could see the shingle hanging out on the building now. "Longshore Realtors." It was going to be epic.

Chapter 6

Caleb thought he was enjoying himself too much. It was like they were thieves in the middle of the night or someone skipping out on their rent and having to move quickly. Cain had had to stifle his own laughter several times as he'd taken his suitcases out of the house and into the back yard, where people were loading them into the van that Caleb had rented just for this. Elly was having a wonderful time writing the note to her dad too.

"I want him to know we no longer need his help, as we're working for ourselves. I'm a little afraid about this, but I'm excited too. Cain always has had the biggest sales when it came to commission checks. Then my dad started taking half of that for wear and tear on the house we were paying too much rent for." Caleb hadn't been happy about that either. Knowing they were paying nearly two grand a month for a falling-down one-bedroom place was appalling. "He'll be upset, but I frankly don't care. Dad will have to get over it. Or not. I'm well past him dictating to me what I should and shouldn't be doing."

By the time everyone was too exhausted to move, the couple was in their own home. As a housewarming gift, Tabby had found them a cook and someone to help clean the house. It was too big a home, she thought, for Elly to do it alone with a baby on the way. Since Caleb owned the house outright, he'd opted for them to rent to own. They were both very happy with that idea.

He also liked the idea of the realtor business. Even if the two of them didn't buy and sell around here much, he was sure he could use them on deals all over the world. He told Cain he would pay for him to get his international licenses, as well as Elly taking a few law classes so she could update her resume. She had been an attorney for a larger firm when her father had demanded that she be at home nightly for him to pop by for a meal when he wanted it. The man was a piece of work, Caleb thought. And he deserved whatever happened when he found out that his children, as he called them, had left the roost, so to speak.

Sitting at his desk at ten-thirty, Caleb was feeling less overwhelmed about the move and other things he had going on at the moment. Today had been the first time in as far back as he could remember that he'd slept later than six in the morning. It had been great that he'd been exhausted, not from stress, but from actual physical labor.

Just as he was thinking about heading up to bed, Tabby came into the room wearing what he could only assume was one of his shirts. He had to swallow twice before he was able to ask her if she needed anything.

"I do, as a matter of fact. I was wondering if sometime tomorrow afternoon, not too early, the two of us could go look for a ring. Unless you have one of your mother's. I don't want to take anything from her, but it would be a pleasure for me to wear one of hers. It would be like she's with us all the time." He asked her what the second thing was. "How did you know there was a second thing, Caleb?"

She shimmied — not walked, but shimmied

over to where he was sitting at the desk. Pulling his chair away from the large oak treasure, he waited for her to make the next move. Caleb didn't have long to wait. Tabby sat up on the desk, her feet on either side of his thighs, and leaned back.

"You are naked beneath that shirt." Smiling, she told him she was so happy he noticed. "I notice a great many things about you. How your breasts make me want to suckle them. The way your ankles look when you're wearing high heels. I don't think women know or realize how much they can get from a man by simply wearing a pair of those."

"Or perhaps we do." He nodded and lifted the shirt up off her breasts and stood up to take one of them into his mouth. "Yes, that's what I need. You to make me come so hard I can't see."

Her breast molded to his mouth. Suckling on the tip, he nipped at the large bud even as he pulled his belt from his pants. Toeing his shoes off, he nearly came when she rubbed her foot over his cock through his pants. Letting her have her way, Caleb pulled his shirt up and over his head. Then he undid his pants around her wandering feet as he watched her pussy get wetter and wetter for him.

"I have a red pair too. They go with this little red dress I got some time back. I've not had much of an opportunity to wear it. Will you eat me, Caleb? I want to feel your mouth over me."

Naked himself, his boxers, which were down around his ankles, slipped off his feet as he sat down in his chair again. Caleb pulled her forward on his desk, so she was just on the very edge. Watching her, slowing moving toward her heat, he saw her eyes close over when he licked her from gate to clit.

"Yes."

She came, flooding his mouth and desktop with her juices. Caleb lapped at her, catching as much as he could as she rode his mouth. When he slid his finger into her, she cried out again, making his own body react hard to the sounds she was making for him.

He couldn't get enough of her. Every time she begged him to stop, to give her a breath, he would slide another finger into her. Flick his tongue over her hard nub until she cried out again. Finally, when she pulled his hair, yanking him from her pussy, he thought that if he died right then, he'd be the most satisfied person in the world. She looked delicious.

"Fuck me." He nodded his head, his cock, hard with the need to come, moving near her. She told him again, her body humming with her need, "Come inside of me, Caleb. Make me scream with a climax that brings the house down. Please. I need to feel you."

Sliding into her slowly, he suckled at her breasts. Her throat and mouth. Each time he thought she couldn't take any more of him, she would move, just enough so he would slide deeper, pull out longer. When he was buried as tightly as he could be inside of her, Caleb gathered her into his arms and lifted her from the desk and sat down on the chair.

"Yes, ride me." She did, her rhythm off a little, but she soon got the hang of it. As he enjoyed her body, holding to her ass and feasting on her breasts, she came over and over. Picking her up again, he took her hard, relentlessly pounding her on the desk until she came several more times. His own pleasure nearly forgotten in watching hers. Caleb was caught so unawares when he did finally release that he was blinded for several seconds as his body emptied deeply into her body.

When he woke, they were both seated in the chair again. Caleb vaguely remembered doing that, taking Tabby with him as they started to slide off the desk. Holding her in his arms now, he watched her sleep. Her naked body was bruised in several places. Her breasts were pinked up as well. While he watched her, gently taking the hair off her forehead, she looked up at him and smiled.

"You ruined me. For anyone." He said that had been his plan all along. "Good. You did it perfectly. If you're not too tired, can you carry me up to bed and sleep with me?"

"I don't think that is even remotely possible. I can barely think about walking myself." She giggled, and he smiled at her. "I do have something for you. But it's all the way over there on my desk. Well, I guess all over the floor now. If I can convince you to stand up on your own, I'll get it for you. Otherwise, we're going to be found here in the morning, naked and sleeping like two people that made love all night."

She giggled again, and he thought he could get used to the sound. Even as she stood, Tabby swayed a little, and he held her steady as he stood himself. Christ, he felt like he'd been drained of every drop of blood, muscle, and bone in the last hour. Walking to the other side of his desk where everything had ended up, he picked up the box he'd had delivered to him while he'd been in town.

"This *was* my mom's, so you know. She told me that her great-grandma had left it to her when she turned sixteen. It's wonderful that you had mentioned you'd like to wear one of hers." He pulled the ring from the jeweler's box and got down on one knee. "Pardon me for being naked, but since this is how I'd like to see you every day, I'm fine with proposing to you like this if you are. Tabitha Jane Tillman, will you marry me? Make this house a home with me? And will you have children with me? I know we didn't discuss that part of it yet, but if you can see your way clear, I'd like to—"

"Shut up, Caleb, so I can tell you yes." He put the ring on her finger. "Oh, it's perfect. And it fits. Yes, I'll marry you. Oh, Caleb, yes. I love you."

He kissed her hand and looked at the ring on her finger. "She didn't wear it much. I think she was afraid of losing it. It's insured if you wish to wear it all the time. I would love for you to do that." She asked him if he was going to ask her about having children. "Yes. I'd like as many as you would like to have."

"I'd love to have one soon. I mean, neither of us is getting any younger, you know." He stood up then, hugging her. Holding her, he realized he'd just proposed to Tabby naked and that he was getting chilled. "How about something to eat? I mean, more than just snack foods. I could eat a steak as big as your head."

"You're a romantic, Tabby. Anyone ever tell you that?" She shook her head. "I wonder why? You have such a way with words, you know."

They ended up taking a shower together. Making love was fun under the water. Also, when she scrubbed his back, some of the muscles that had been sore before started to loosen up. Doing the same for her, he told her about the building he was working on. And the issue he was having with the CEO's suite of offices on the second floor.

"Aren't they normally on, like, the top floor? I mean so that the little peons below him have to be impressed with him." He laughed and told her what he knew of the building owners. "Oh, so this is a not-for-profit kind of thing. I would think they'd be better off using some of the empty buildings around their town. That way, the money going for this project would be better spent."

"Yes, then I'd not be getting paid. However, I did bring that up to him. He told me that the people, I don't know who he might have been talking about, want him to be in a better building. I suppose he's right on that. The town voted for the building to be put in. There is one thing to remember in this. He will employ a great many people to work there. As well as the construction crew that I'll be working with is all local men and woman."

"Still." Caleb knew she was right. He'd been thinking the same thing since he'd been asked to design his first not-for-profit building. "All right. I'm ready. How about we decide what stuff has to be done today, and we work our meal around that? I have a meeting with Kylie at noon with the board of directors. She said they just want to meet me, and Sheppard would be there too. Do you realize when we're married, he'll be my grandfather-in-law?"

Caleb stood in their bedroom for several minutes, just thinking on relationships. Tabby hadn't meant anything by her words. He was sure of that. But it made it no less heart aching to know that his mom wasn't there to meet his soon-to-be bride. He did wonder how she'd feel about his relationship with her parents. He thought it was high time that he spoke to both of them, just to see what they thought of him just being around. Perhaps, he thought again, he should have asked them before selling everything he owned and moving into their area.

~*~

Dick was giving them time to beg him to come over and be with them. Wanting them to suffer a little, he'd not been by the house or spoken to them in three days now. Not since he'd caught them moving the upstart into his home. Also, to get back at them, he'd been firing off emails to them on how things were going to go from now on.

He'd doubled their rent last night, sending the notification by email. Also, he decided that he was going to add onto the house they were in and make himself a room there. It would have to be larger than theirs. Also, he'd have a bathroom of his own.

Elly wouldn't have to bring his laundry back and forth from her home to his when she did it. Of course, they would have to go to the laundromat when there was washing to be done. He wouldn't allow one of those things in any of his rentals, as they wasted water. Not that he paid for water. He just collected, not paid for shit. Also, he thought it wore out the electrical components faster, and he wasn't going to be paying for new wiring in a house that he didn't live in.

The knock at his door brought him from his planning.

"Mr. Douglas, Mr. Shimer is here to see you. He said it's important." Dick told his employee to send him in. "Yes, sir."

Dick didn't learn their names until they had a huge sale come in. The only person whose name he had remembered was Cain's, as it turned out. Cain was their top salesman every month. Not that he gave him anything for it. He was, after all, his son-in-law and his renter.

"Did you know there is another bank going into town? I had to find out from one of the people working for me." Dick told Slam he'd not heard that, but he didn't see a problem with it. "No problem. Are you insane? It's a huge fucking problem. How the hell do you think I'll be able to fund our little outings if some of the people with loans at the bank go down the street? And you know they will when word gets out about how they're getting a better interest rate from them."

"You don't think whoever is coming here can be paid off? I do. Everyone has their price. Once they hire someone to run it, we'll just go and have a little talk with him. Whoever it turns out to be, it'll be someone else that we have in our pockets." Slam sat down. "I don't suppose you've seen Cain or Elly out and about, have you? I had to have a little talk with them the other day, and I'm waiting for them to come to my terms on things. I'm still working on getting those purchases reversed that Cain sold. The little fucker not only sold him the land but the Bundy property too."

"I bet that was a nice payoff for you." Dick only shook his head. "You didn't give it all to him, did you? That's not like you at all, Dick. Are you getting soft now that you have a grandson coming along?"

"That attorney for the kid that bought everything, he came in here with the bill of sales and demanded the check for the commissions for Cain. I haven't any idea how he knew just how much Cain should have gotten. Cain isn't stupid enough to tell anyone what the going rate is. Not without consequences. Anyway, I had to write him out a check for the entire amount before I got my check as his boss. Mother fucker. He'd better know I'm going to be getting that back from him too. No one plays me that way."

It had nearly reduced him to tears when he'd had to write out the check for Cain. Dick should have, as he'd always done, gotten half of it, even after his commission on being the realtor. But no, the guy had to make sure that Cain got his full amount. And the fucking attorney had made him get a cashier's check too. There wasn't any way he could cancel payment on it.

"I'm thinking that when Cain does come back, and it'll be any day now, I'm going to have to cut his wages a bit more. There isn't any way he's going to get by with thinking he made out on a deal that I told him not to do. Damn it." Slam asked him how he was going to pay his rent if he took more money from him—not that he cared, he told him. "That will make him all the more beholden to me. I told Elly he was worthless and not to marry him. But they ran off like thieves in the night and did it. Now I'm having to make sure they have a roof over their heads, and they pay their rent on time."

"You're a hard ass, Dick. I think that's what I admire so much about you. How you have the balls to do just about anything you fucking want." Slam snapped his fingers. "I just remembered something. Did you know that Shep is working a full-time job now? Christ, what is this world coming to when the richest kid in the state is laying bricks for a living? I bet his parents are so proud of him too."

"You know the Andersons—they more than likely are proud of him. He was a hellraiser for a while there. They're incredibly stupid if you ask me. Forever bitching about one thing or another." Dick had a thought. "You don't suppose they're related to that newcomer, do you? He's Anderson too, right?"

"I doubt it. I saw them the other day out someplace. The younger one calls him Mr. Anderson, as well as calling Melissa Mrs. Anderson. That is a strange man if you ask me.

He just shows up out of nowhere, buys up all the land that we were holding onto, then has his attorney going around asking questions." Dick asked what sort of questions he was asking. "Mostly to the underwhelming people in town. The downtrodden and shit like that. He was taking a survey on how many people rented as to how many owned their own homes. I don't think any of them own shit. However, I was thinking that they do rent from you. A great many of them, as a matter of fact, right?"

"Yes. I'd say all, but there have been a few holdouts in selling me their places. But I'll get around to it." The knock at his door had him shushing Slam when he started to speak again. "Yes, what is it now?"

"I can't get through to your line, sir. So I had the gentleman call you on your cell. We're making calls from our cells out here now as the phones aren't working at all. And no Internet." He told him to get onto that. "I am. I just said that I was."

The door shut before he could fire the young man. There was no hope for any of them to makes any sales this week if no one could call them. Not that there was much buying and selling going on right now. The town was dead as far as he was concerned. Picking up the phone when it rang, he was dismayed to see that it was a private number.

"This is Sheppard Alexander, Dick. I'd like to speak to you about a couple of matters." Dick sat up higher in his chair just as he realized that the man couldn't see him. He asked him what he could do for him. "Nothing. I was just speaking to my new attorney here. It seems I've been remiss in a few things. I'm sure you don't care to hear about all of them. But I did want to point out that I own the property your business is sitting on. Were you aware of that?"

"I was. It's the perfect piece of property for our business, sir. We have a nice view of the streets and the comings and goings of the town." Confused a little, Dick waited to see what the man would say next. When he didn't say anything else, Dick, as usual, felt the need to fill in the silence. "I was thinking of calling you next month about having new carpet put into the place. It's worn in a couple of places that are beginning to be a hazard to the people that work for me."

"I'm having the place torn down in thirty

days. As for the carpet, I'm not going to put any in if I'm going to demolish it. I'm sure you can understand that." Dick asked him where he was going to set up shop. "Well, I'm not sure that's any of my concern, are you? I mean, as far back as before my son was out of high school, you stopped paying me any sort of rent. I'm not going to sue you for back rent now, though I more than likely would win. Instead, so that it's not something that slips my mind again with you, I'm having the building torn down and a nicer one put in its place."

"Would it be a place we could rent from you? The reason I ask, I have ten people working for me that will be out of work should I have to fire them." Mr. Anderson asked him if he thought that was his fault. "Well, you are tearing down their means of support." He asked him to hang on a moment. When Anderson came back on the line only after the briefest of moments, he was laughing.

"You have three employees, Dick, one of them being you. As for them being unemployed, I'm reasonably sure they're about hitting poverty now with what you pay them. Do you really take money from them to advertise? That's highway robbery." He had only a second to wonder how he'd heard that before he spoke again. "No, I'm not going to rent the new place to you. I think the people around town might be better off working for someone else than you. From what I'm hearing, there will be a couple of new businesses coming along here soon anyway."

"Really? Where did you hear that?" Instead of answering him, the man simply hung up on him. "He's tearing down the building. Not only that, but he's not going to rent the new place to me. What the hell is going on around here, Slam? Why are things suddenly going to shit for me?"

"For us. Now I'm doubly worried about the new bank coming in. I might have to go back to my office and find out who owns the land the building is sitting on. Christ, this is terrible." As he stood up, his phone was ringing. "Unknown. Could be Anderson again. I'm not answering it until I have information. I'll see you later, Dick. Let me know if there are any newer developments going on."

Dick was still sitting there when his cell phone rang again. Instead of answering it, he let it go to voice mail. This was bullshit. He did have a moment, wondering if this was even legal. But then Anderson did say he'd spoken to his new attorney. Putting his head in his hands on his desk, he tried to think past that he wasn't going to be able to find a place to open shop. People would demand that he pay them rent, not to mention, he'd have to move all the shit he had here.

It was a quarter past two when he finally got up from his desk to see what he could salvage. Also, he figured it was high time that he went to see his daughter. He might be moving in with her quicker than he thought.

Dick had never been one to save money. If he had it, it was as good as spent. Even with all the money coming in that he was making off the sales that Cain made, he was forever bouncing a check or two. Or his credit card that was directly attached to his account would not have enough on it to cover his lunch or other expenses.

As soon as he was in the outer office, he knew something was really wrong. The lights were all off. Testing one of the switches, he knew the power was on, but there was just no one working. Going to the five cubicles he'd slapped together when the sales crew was doing more socializing than making calls, there wasn't anything on the desks either. No pens. Not a single paperclip was to be found. Even opening the drawers to see if they were simply people that cleaned up after themselves, he found them to be empty as well. What the hell was going on here?

It took him twenty minutes to find out that his car, which was another rental that he didn't pay for, was gone. Heading to the police station to file a claim, he was stopped by Slam again. He had all his things from his desk in a box and was carrying it out of the bank. He asked him what was going on.

"I've been terminated as of the second I got back to the office. There were Feds there, Dick. They've closed down the bank to do an audit, and then they'll reopen in a few weeks. But regardless, I've been fired." He asked under what grounds they could do that. "Misappropriation of funds. Poor work performance. That's from the head office. Theft. Property damage. Falsifying company records. Christ, they had a list longer than my arm. They told me I'm not to leave town or they're going to hunt me down. Dick, I'm going to prison."

"Prison? What the hell have you been

doing there, Slam? I mean, they can't have figured out our little plot, can they?" Slam just looked back at the bank, then at him. "Slam, did you tell them?"

"I had to. I had to tell them everything."

Dick was still standing there when a car beeped at him. Dick hadn't realized he'd been standing in the middle of the road until that moment. Dick made his way to his daughter's home. He needed a place to hide out and to think. Also, he figured Elly would have some money from the commission's check. It wasn't like they were going to need it worse than he was. Dick needed to get out of the country right fucking now. She'd better not give him any shit either.

By the time he made it to her house, it was late. There were police everywhere he'd gone. Dick hadn't even been able to get himself a cup of coffee, something he needed to calm himself down enough to think. He'd been all over this town, moving in and out of alleys to get where he wanted to go.

All the lights were off in the place, and he realized he'd forgotten his keys at work. Oh well, whoever had taken his car, they'd not be getting far without the keys, he thought. Knocking, then pounding on the door, nothing stirred. It wasn't until the woman next door came out of her place to tell him to be quiet that he was able to figure out some things. He asked her where his daughter was.

"Moved out." He told her that wasn't possible, that he'd not given her permission for that. "Yet she's gone and done it. I don't know how long it's been since you looked at your daughter, Dick, but I'd say she's not had to ask you for permission for shit for a long time. They ain't nobody there. Now get on out of here before I call the cops on you."

He asked her where they'd gone, but the woman had closed her door and ears to him now. Dick was afraid she would call the police, and all his shimming around the town would have been for nothing. Not sure what to do now, he headed to the last place he'd seen the two of them. Maybe the person there would tell him where they'd gone.

"Ungrateful shits. After all I've done for them." He'd actually done nothing and knew it. But this was his child, and she'd better damned well step up and help him. Or else. He hadn't any idea what sort of threat he could hold over them, but— "They went and spent that money on buying their way out of living in that house. Mother fuck. They had better not have spent it all. I'm not kidding right now."

By the time he was at the house, he was exhausted. The lights there were turned off too, but he didn't bother with trying to get in. Waiting till tomorrow might well keep his ass from getting shot up. He didn't know who might be living in the house. It could well have been the Anderson man, but he wasn't sure. Waiting until morning seemed like a good idea.

Dick took the blanket off the chair on the front porch and made himself a little bed with the swing out there. Elly would have to beg for him not to be to upset with her after this. After all, she was supposed to be daddy's little girl. That sent him into peals of laughter that lasted until he fell into a deep sleep.

Chapter 7

Joey didn't have anything left. Nothing in his heart, his mind, or even his body. Everything he'd ever had, hoped for, or even wished for was gone. He was no different, no better than the hundreds of other homeless veterans across this country. Picking up his service weapon, he laid it in his lap while he tried to figure out where was the best place to end his life.

It wasn't the place he was concerned about. It would be days, if not longer, before anyone were to find his body. Should he put the gun in his mouth? His temple? Perhaps in his belly. Not that he thought he could suffer any more than he was now, but there was the off chance he'd live through it and be in worse shape than he was currently.

Two weeks ago, the plant he'd been working in closed up. They had moved, they told all the people working there, to a place that would cut them better deals on taxes. That if they had a beef about it, to take it up with the government of their town. Joey, like sixty other employees, was denied unemployment. He'd have to take it up with his previous employers, as they were the ones that hadn't paid into unemployment for any of them.

"You got anything to eat, Big Joe?" He told the man next to him that his name was Joey, not Joe. "Oh, really? Well, you got anything to eat? I sure could use a cookie or two about now. I'm pretty near starving."

He'd talked to this man every day for the last two weeks. Joey told him not just his name but also that he was a war veteran, that his mom had passed on, and that he was looking for a job. Nothing was out there much if you didn't have an address where you lived.

"I don't have anything to eat, Sherman. I'm sorry about that. I've not eaten for a few days myself." Sherman nodded but didn't move, not before asking if he had anything to eat. "No. Try the soup kitchen."

"I'll do that. Do you know where it is?" He pointed down the street, knowing that Sherman wouldn't be able to find it even if he had someone guiding him there. Sherman had hit the needle a few too many times, and it had fried his brain cells. "Thanks, Big Joe."

Why on earth he could remember what he didn't want to be called and not his name was a mystery to him. There were others around here like that. Martha, he thought her name was, had been pushing a stroller around since he'd seen her with a doll in it. She must have lost a child at some point, and it messed with her mind. Martha treated the doll that she had better than Joey had seen people treat their real kids.

"Joseph Phillips?" He looked up but didn't say that was his name to the two men that were standing next to a cardboard box asking for him. "We're looking for Sergeant Joseph Phillips. Does anyone know him?"

"There ain't no Phillip around here, mister. You got any food on you? Something I can have. I am hungry." The man whistled, and someone came toward them with a huge box. The two men, with the woman now with them, started handing out not just bags of food but blankets too. "Oh, my goodness. It's food. And it's warm too. Lookee here, Big Joe. Food for us."

The woman came to him first. "I don't know why you're looking for me, but I've nothing to say to you. I'm not interested in becoming a lab rat, nor am I willing to kill anyone for you."

"You get that a lot down here, Joey?" He nodded and looked up at her. "I'm not here for any of those things, honestly. But here is some food for you while we— Your gun slipped. Let me get it for you."

Before he could guess what she was about to do, not only was his gun picked up, but she had put it in the back of her pants. He asked her to give it back to him.

"It's about the only possession I have." She sat down on the ground with him, unmindful of her clothing or the fact that he was someone she didn't know. "What is it you want, ma'am? A good lay? Sorry. I don't think that even in better places, I'd be able to satisfy anyone. I've already asked about the other things that people usually want. Tell me what it is you want from me so I can turn you down, and you'll go away."

"Your father was Howard Berkley." He didn't say a word. Not that he was shocked by her knowing, but that she'd bring that up. "My husband is one of his bastards too. His mom, like yours, passed away recently, and she set him on the task of finding the men that Berkley fathered. You're just one of six, I'm afraid to say."

"He's dead then." She nodded. "Okay. Good to know. Now I won't have to go to prison for ending his life. However, it might have been a little better living conditions than I have now. Did you come here to tell me that? Thanks. Anything else before you head out?"

"Yes. As I said, Caleb has been tasked to find you five. Abby, Caleb's mother, wanted him to help you guys in any way he could. If you allow us to, we'll take you home with us and get you healthy again. After that, we'll figure out where to go from there."

"I don't need — well, I don't want your help. I want my gun back so I can do what I wanted to do before you got here." She held out the gun, but before he could reach for it, she took it back, slammed a bullet into the chamber, and gave it back to him. "You think you're so smart? You're not. You just might have given a man his death by handing that back. What happens if you read in the paper tomorrow that I offed myself?"

"Would it be more helpful if I were to shoot you?" She snatched the gun back and held it to his head. "No one would notice you being dead. By the time they did, your body would be rolled and picked over. All evidence of me doing it would be gone. Not to mention, my prints wouldn't even be on the bullet. They're all yours. Then there is the sad fact that it's doubtful anyone would be around to mourn your death."

"You're a bitch." The man that came to stand behind the woman told him to watch himself. "Did you hear what she just said to me? That she would kill me, and no one would care."

"Would they? I mean, like she said, who would even know that you were here until it was too late?" Joey stood up and then realized that the man was just a little taller than he was. Also, he noticed that whoever he was, he wasn't afraid of him. "You and I have the same colored eyes and hair. My mom was a blonde. Seventeen when Berkley took advantage of her. How old was your mom?"

"Sixteen. Seventeen when she had me. How do you know? Why are you doing this?" Caleb, he assumed his name was, told him what the woman had. "So, you're doing this as a promise to your mother? How will she ever know if you do it or not? I mean, mine wouldn't."

"I would know." Joey could understand that as well. "Come with us. Please? I have a few things I'd like to talk to you about."

"Caleb, I presume." He nodded. "I have nothing. Less than nothing. I haven't any idea why I think you have it all, but there isn't any way you can help me out that would have much of a lasting effect on my life. Not unless you can give me a good job that I'll work hard at. A nice suit to wear to work that I'll pay you back for, as well as a place I can call my own. That's really all I want in life."

"Deal." Caleb put out his hand. "You set the terms that I'm willing to meet for you to come with me. A deal is a deal, Joey. Shake on it, and we'll get moving."

He looked around at the men and women he'd been with over the last few days. They were all wrapped up in blankets. Warm food and a warm, dry place to sleep was good for that. He looked back at the couple.

"They're going to need more than a one-time shot here. You are aware of that, aren't you?" He said he was and what he'd done to improve their lots in life. "How long will that last, Caleb? Until some other shiny thing comes along—" Joey was appalled at himself. "I'm sorry. I had no right to say that. I've been so long without social needs that I forget myself."

"You're fine. And yes, they need more than a one-time shot. But as I said, I've given enough money to the right people that will have food brought to them once a day. For those that are willing, jobs will be provided as well. Nothing too difficult, but something that can get them a start."

He was getting into a limo when he realized he had no idea where they were going. Before he could begin to worry that he might well have made a mistake, the car was pulling up in front of a hotel.

Usually, he was stopped before entering such an establishment. Today he was not only asked if he needed anything extra in his room but also told that a man would be up directly to measure him for some clothing. The room he was led to was a suite. It had a nice kitchen, a huge bathroom, as well as a nice set of brand new luggage sitting empty on the extra bed.

Caleb knocked on the door as Joey was

looking in the full-sized refrigerator. Letting him in as he drank a bottle of water, Caleb handed him a file. Joey nearly told him he had figured this would happen, that there was a catch when the other man spoke.

"I know you lost your mother, and I wanted to tell you how very sorry that I am. My mom passed away recently too. The paperwork there is telling you that your mom's hospital bills are paid, as well as her funeral costs. Also, I have an attorney looking into why you and the others were denied unemployment. That should have been yours from the start since they closed up and didn't fire you guys first." Joey sat down. The knock at the door had Caleb telling him that he'd get it. "This is Shawn. He's going to take your measurements to get you some clothing to wear. I'm assuming you don't have any stashed anywhere?"

"Nothing." Shawn didn't say a word as he took his measurements and wrote them down. Caleb was still talking when the man asked him for his shoe size. "Eleven wide."

"I'm to understand that you were in security in the service. I have an opening at the plant my wife is running. Well, she's not my wife yet. In the morning, we're headed to the courthouse to get that taken care of. Anyway, I want her watched over, and I'd like you to make sure we're not missing something that will get her hurt."

"This is a real job you're giving me?" Caleb said he'd not become a wealthy man by given fake jobs to people. "You're wealthy. I guess I could have guessed that on my own, but I'm assuming for some reason that wealthy is a gross understatement for you and your soon-to-be wife."

"You'd be correct. I have someone looking for the other men that were found to be sired by Berkley. I want you to know that if he weren't dead, he would have been soon. However, it's all water under the bridge now, and I'm going to do my damnest to make sure his sons aren't suffering because he couldn't keep his dick in his pants." Joey laughed, asking Caleb if he was normally so outspoken. "No. I think Tabby is rubbing off on me a little."

"She is a pistol. Speaking of which, I didn't get mine back from her." Caleb stood up and pulled the weapon out of the back of his pants. "You're assuming I will no longer use it on myself."

"We made a deal, which we've yet to shake on. However, I can wait. I also can understand why you're unbelieving of me not wanting anything in return for how we're helping you. That's fine too. We'll get there." Joey had a feeling they would too. Even if he went into it kicking and screaming all the way. "There is a house for you to live in. Before you tell me that you don't need a home, you will. I want you to be able to stretch out and have an office at your home, as well as one where Tabby is working. Also, there are a couple of other properties I might need you to have a look at. My grandparents', as well as my uncle's home. Wealthy men come with crazy ideas from people trying to make a buck off them."

"What are you getting out of this, Caleb? I mean, it seems to me that you're putting a great deal on the line for a man you know very little about." He told him. Joey had to sit down. "Brother. You're my half-brother."

"I don't believe in doing a job halfway, Joey, so as far as I'm concerned, we're brothers. As will be the other four when I find them." Caleb stood up and smiled at him. "My wife is resting right now, or she'd be here making sure you're eating well, having a nice long shower to warm you up, as well as a good night's sleep. If I were you, I'd at least tell her that you're doing all right in the morning, or she'll be all over you for it. I love her very much, but you'll see that she's extremely outspoken and a mother hen all at the same time."

"You really do love her that much." Caleb said he loved her with all his heart. "That's a wonderful thing to have. I hope you know that."

"Yes, I do." He went to the door. "Oh, there is a cell phone on the table for you. It's programmed with mine and my wife's number already. It's yours to use however you wish. Also, there are several cards next to it with the numbers of my attorney should you like to talk to him, as well as my grandparents. They know you might call them. Goodnight, Joey. Sleep well."

Going to get the phone, just to see what sort it was, he laughed when he realized he should have guessed it would be state of the art. Along with the numbers that were there, a large, wrapped gift was there as well. He opened it up when he saw that someone had put his name on the little tag.

A laptop, brand new, that was also very high tech. Putting it back in the box so he'd not get wrapped up in playing with it, Joey took the long shower that was suggested to him. Using the products there that also had his name on them, he wrapped a large fluffy towel around his waist and went to the bedroom. All of a sudden, he was bone-tired and laid on the bed. Joey thought he was asleep long before his eyes had the chance to catch up with his body.

~*~

"I'm sorry to have kept you waiting." Caleb was rushing into the office when Sheppard stood up. "I stayed up late last night working on a project, and I overslept. I know that Tabby set the alarm for me, and it's unlike me to—"

"It's all right, Caleb. Your lovely cook gave me some tea and a few biscuits, and I'm just fine. Melissa is on her way. She's running behind as well. I'm to understand that you found one of the men that were fathered by the same man you were." He said they'd gone to get him the day before yesterday. They both sat down. "Good for you. I have to tell you that Tabby is doing a fine job with the business. I got a phone call just yesterday from the plant security manager telling me that she's hired someone to look after her and us. I don't know that we'll need all that. We've not had any trouble like that before."

"That's one of the many reasons I wanted to talk to the two of you." Melissa joined them a few minutes after tea and some biscuits were brought in for him too. "I feel horrible about all this. Why don't we head to the living room, and we'll be a good deal more comfortable there."

As soon as they were seated, thankfully, Tabby showed up. He told her what had happened, and she kissed him anyway. They'd been having a blast since they were married, and he was happy every second that they'd not made a big deal about it.

"As you know, Mom and I worked very hard to get ourselves a place in this life. Mom had a great head on her shoulders for a great many things, as I'm sure you know, and she could invest in people on sight. It's what made us so wealthy." Sheppard said he knew about hard work and saving money. "I know you do. However, what you don't know, and it's a very well-kept secret, is just how wealthy we are. As I said, Mom was good at investments, and between the two of us working hard, we're billionaires. Tabby and I are worth well over two hundred billion dollars."

He watched the two of them as they absorbed that. Caleb knew the precise moment when it hit them that he'd not said million, but billion. Sheppard stood up and sat down twice before he asked him if he was serious.

"I am. The reason I'm telling you that is not to brag but to make you understand why there is a need for bodyguards on us at all times. I don't want anything to happen to my family, in the event someone gets it in their head that taking any of you from me will get him money." Melissa asked him if he considered them family now. "That's another thing I've wanted to talk to you about. I've been a selfish prick in not acknowledging you as being my grandparents. Tabby pointed out the error of my ways several times over the last few days. She's very painful when she has something to get across."

"We don't need you to agree to be our grandson because you were bullied into it, Caleb." Caleb told him it didn't matter, really, as he was their grandson. "You are willing to call us that? You don't have to. Just knowing that you think it is enough for me."

"It's no longer enough for me. Grandda." His grandfather started sobbing, holding onto his grandma while she cried as well. "I hope you can understand where I was coming from when I first arrived. But since then, I should have taken steps to make sure you knew that I no longer felt that way. That for as much as I'm sure you missed my mom, you missed out on me as well. I'd very much like to get to know you and for you to know me. And any children that Tabby and I have."

"We were married a couple of days ago. Neither of us wanted to have a big deal made out of it, so there wasn't any backlash in the papers for any of us." Grandda stood up and jerked him up from the couch while Tabby laughed. The hug he received would stay with him forever, he thought. It was, Caleb thought, the first time he'd ever been hugged by a man. He was happy that it was his grandfather that had done it. "I guess you're okay with this."

Tabby was hugged as well. The four of them cried a little and hugged several more times before they were seated again. Even then, Grandma got up and sat on his other side and took his hand into hers as he continued to talk.

"Tabby has decided to keep her maiden name for now at the plant. Mostly because she didn't want people thinking what people normally do when a woman takes over the running of a huge company. I'd like to if you would work with me, make Anderson's a much larger and more diverse company than it is now. Do more of the things you've started with helping the public." Grandda thought it was a wonderful idea. "We'll work together, the four of us. And when Shep is settled more — I think he'll be getting married soon too — we'll have him brought in to be a part of it. We can do so much by working together."

It was nearly lunch when they were finished talking about the business aspect of the meeting. Caleb had told them of some of the investments he'd been able to make and invited his grandparents to enjoy the benefits of the homes he owned abroad.

"Your mom would be so proud of you, Caleb." He told his grandma that all he thought about was doing himself proud for her. "I miss her, you know. But having you here, it's made things seem so wonderful. To see her through you. My goodness, I miss her so much at times that I want to go find her."

"She's in a good place. Mom suffered terribly when she was in the end stages of her cancer." He changed the subject then when he saw how much it had hurt Grandma. "Tabby is wearing the ring that Mom got from...I think your mother when she turned sixteen. She said she loved it but was afraid of losing it."

"Yes, I remember that ring. It looks so lovely on you, Tabby." They talked about everything and really nothing at all as they had lunch. Just as they were finishing up, Shep joined them with Kylie, and he was brought up to speed on the things that were going on. "They're married, Shep. Isn't that wonderful?"

"Yes, it is. Kylie has agreed to marry me. I knew you'd be here, and I wanted to come by and tell you the good news. I don't mean to rain on your parade, Caleb. I should have waited." Caleb told him he was happy that they told him. "Thanks. Without you and Tabby doing what you did, I don't think I would ever have been as happy as I am right now."

Cain called him just as he was sitting down with his family. "You have time to come over here? I told you about Dick being on the porch the other morning, right?"

"Yes. You said you had the police roust him out. Has he returned?" Cain said he had and that he'd taken Elly. "I'll be right there, Cain. Stay at the house, and I'll be there in a few minutes."

"I don't know what to do, Caleb. She's all I have in the world." Caleb assured him that he'd find him, or the police would. "Please hurry. I need someone to keep me upright."

They were headed to the house and pulling into the drive just as the police showed up. Cain was a mess, and he was also beaten up quite a bit. After calling an ambulance, the police sat down with Cain as Kylie and Arthur sat on either side of him. He was going to need an attorney before this was over, simply so he'd not be blamed for anything happening to Dick. And something would happen if Caleb had anything to say about it.

"We were having breakfast when the back door just exploded open. He didn't hesitate at all but fired at Melody, our new cook and killed her. When his gun jammed up, he started picking up things around the kitchen and hitting me with them. I had shoved Elly out of the room at some point, but when I was hit over the head with something and was out, he must have found her. What am I going to do?" The police assured him they'd find them. Caleb noticed that no one was saying she'd be alive. That scared him more than anything. "What is it you're not telling me? There's more than him just taking my wife, isn't there? Tell me. Please?"

"He killed Mr. Shimer last night. The FBI was looking for Douglas when they came across Mr. Shimer's body. He'd been beaten badly before being shot in the head." Grandma hugged Cain as Sher, the officer, continued. "I'm not saying for sure that Douglas did it, but we have reason to believe he might well be involved in two other murders as well."

"Why? I mean, can you tell us that?" Caleb nodded when Sher told him that he couldn't. "I see. All right. What is it that is being done? I mean, to find him. Anything I or any of us can do to help?"

"Not at the moment, no. Now we have to find him before anyone else gets hurt." Tabby asked Sher if he'd checked the house that Cain and his wife had been living in. "I didn't know there was anywhere else. Can you tell me where that is?"

After giving him the information, Sher called it into the Feds. They were better equipped to handle this situation, and he was out of his league, he told them. Almost as soon as he hung up the phone, it rang again. It was Douglas, and he was asking for the ingrate son-in-law.

Cain put the phone on speaker as he was directed. Douglas was ranting about commission checks and how much Cain owed him before he finally got to the point. He wanted money and a great deal of it. Or he'd never see his wife again. Not alive, anyway.

"I want to speak to Elly." Douglas laughed, and Caleb heard the woman screaming. "You fucking prick, she's your daughter. Not to mention she's carrying your grandchild. What the hell is wrong with you? Let her go."

"You'll give me all the money you got from that last sale, or it won't matter one hill of beans what she's doing or how she's related to me. I mean to get out of the country, and you're going to help me. And don't fucking call the cops. I'm having enough trouble with them as it is." Cain was instructed to ask about Slam Shimer. "Well, of course, I killed him, you fucking moron. He told the police about our little deal. Damn it all to fuck and back. I hated doing that too. Slam was the only friend I had, and now he's dead. On account of you. You shouldn't have married my daughter. Nothing would be going to shit if you'd just left us alone."

The line went dead, and no one moved. Grabbing Caleb's grandma, Cain sobbed on her shoulder until he had to be physically taken to the couch before he fell over. It wasn't until Grandma called a doctor that Caleb realized how much he didn't want the same thing to ever happen again. He would keep his family safe at all costs. And take care that Cain's was as well.

Chapter 8

"You've no idea how much I appreciate this, Joey. I know it's terrible of us to only just meet, and now we're asking you to kill a man. You telling us that you were a sniper in the service was about the best news any of us had heard." Joey told Caleb that he'd saved his life. "No. We gave you a help-up. The only life-saving was this. I promise you, you'll not be in any sort of trouble for helping out the police with this." He really hoped not.

Joey didn't mind doing this for the Andersons. It was the Federal officer, Agent Windermere, that was pissing him off. He wanted Douglas alive, at all costs. Windermere said that Douglas had to answer for his crimes, and in order for him to do that, he needed to be alive. Joey wasn't happy with that answer, nor did he care for the man telling him *at all costs.*

"What about the woman? Shouldn't she be able to live too? Not to mention her baby. I mean, she is going to have a child that could very well be the next president or someone nice." Windermere glared at him and repeated that he was to live at all costs. "Are you telling me that if the woman has to die, you're all right with that?"

"Now you're with the program. See that he lives, or I'm not kidding you, young man. I'll make military prison look like a sunny walk in the park." Joey looked at Sher, who only pointed to his vest. He'd completely forgotten there was a camera there. "Now that you see reason, you get your ass up there on that building and make sure you wait for my word before you take the shot. Shoot him in the arm or something, but do not kill him."

When he walked away, Joey decided he'd be better off not doing this. There was just too much at stake here—his life and that of the woman. Before he could do as he wanted, just go back to the Anderson home, Kimble found him. After a quick handshake, he smiled.

Officer Kimble had been polite, even going

so far as to make sure he had the paperwork that would keep him from going to prison for killing a man if it came to that. The fed had told him it wouldn't mean a hell of a lot if he were to fuck this up. There was no doubt in his mind that he'd do what was required of him for this officer, but this was just too messed up, even for non-army orders.

"We've not seen the wife yet, but we know she's alive. The other sniper could see that before he was shot. The moron. Who stands atop a building waving at the guy he's to kill? Anyway, there are only the two people in the house, and so far, we've not been able to breach anything but the front door. He threatens the woman every time. However, since I've not heard anyone tell me that this is their game, meaning Windermere, I'm going to tell you that you are to only listen to me, Joey. I will not throw you under the bus." Joey wasn't so sure about any of this, but Caleb told him that if anyone could be trusted, it would be Sher. "I'm in charge here. I swear to you that no one is going to prison at all if you do what I tell you."

"I'm going to be honest with you when I tell you that I feel like I'm being put in the middle here. I don't mind helping out with this. I like Cain. But I swear to you, I will not put myself on the line for anyone but you." Sher thanked him. "Don't do that yet. That little fucker over there is on a power trip, and he won't care who he has to take down to get what he wants."

"We'll get this." He believed him. "You get yourself set up. You have the ear device that makes it so you can hear me?"

"Yes." Giving him the one that Windermere had given him, Joey put the one from Sher in his ear. "Can you hear me?"

"Loud and clear." Joey hurried across the street to the building across from the house. He was getting the gun set up when he heard from Sher again. "We've had contact with Douglas. He wants money from Cain. Something about a commission check. Windermere is telling him that he can have whatever he wants, that he's as safe as a pig in a blanket. Is it all right to speak to you while you're getting ready?"

"I'm about finished up here anyway. This is a very nice weapon." He had his rifle ready when he looked through the scope. "I wonder where this sucker came from. This is about the best I've ever seen. I wish I'd had time to practice with it, but I don't foresee any troubles. I can see into the house. The woman is on the chair, and Douglas is nowhere to be seen. I see shadows, but not him as yet." Sher told him that Caleb had gotten the gun. "I bet it didn't come cheap either."

He kept a running detail on what he could see in the house. Occasionally he'd look below him and see that everyone was just where they'd been when he left, milling around like they were at some sort of social event. Looking into the house, he could see that the woman was unconscious. Telling Sher that, he asked if she was breathing or not.

"I have no idea what you can see or not, but it would go a long way in making Cain happy to know that his wife is at least breathing." Joey told him he could see her chest moving in and out. Also, she was moving her legs around. "Thank you. Christ, this is a nightmare. All right. I'm to tell you that when you have a clear shot, take him. Dead is what I want, but you do whatever you can to get this finished. Just do it and break down."

Joey watched the man and woman in the house across from him. When Douglas walked by the window, Joey counted until he walked by it again. Pacing was going to give him just what he wanted. When Douglas walked by the fourth time, Joey fired and hit him in the head. Before the man hit the floor, Joey was doing just what he'd been told. Breaking down the rifle and putting it away.

"All clear." He was still breaking down the rifle when he saw Windermere gesturing with his hands. He would point up his way a couple of times but continued to scream at Sher. The Fed was screaming so loudly that while he couldn't hear what he was saying, Joey knew he was pissed off. The voice in his head wasn't Sher but Caleb this time.

"Go to my home as quickly as you can." He said he would and that he would see him there. Joey was packed up and down the stairs to the lowest level when Tabby met him at the back of the building.

"I'm to take you home with me." Nodding, he got into the waiting limo after the rifle was stashed in the trunk. "I owe you a great deal for this, Joey. At great risk for what you had to do, you did it for Cain and the rest of us. I cannot thank you enough."

"I'd like to tell you it was my pleasure, but that sounds like I'm being a dick. I'm not." Tabby told him she knew that. "What happens now? I mean, that fed, he's got a real hard-on for that man being alive. He's not, just so you know."

"Caleb said it was a clean shot. He's going to meet us at the house too. So you know, he's not one to mess with. I'm sure you've figured that out." Joey laughed and said he had. "Good. Also, there is something else I'd like to talk to you about. You're going to be doing security for Caleb and myself in watching over our families. I would very much appreciate it if you were to keep an eye on Cain and his wife. They've come to mean a great deal to me, just as you have. I don't want anything to happen to anyone."

"I'm going to make it my priority to make sure that you and all of them are taken care of. You guys mean a great deal to me as well." She thanked him. "No need for that. I do have a question. What is it that this man did, besides taking this woman? He seemed to be a little off his rocker when he was pacing in the house. By the way, whose house was that?"

"Douglas owned the house. The woman was his daughter." She told him everything. "He also killed the banker who told the police about the little scam they had going on. It's kind of complicated, which means to me that someone else had figured it out. Douglas and a man by the name of Slam were buying up land and planning to use it to lure people here that would pay them great sums of money. However, once they were here, they'd not be able to build without paying for other things that would put them behind. That would be a breach of contract in having a business—I think you get it. No one would have been able to make anything work, so they'd be free to sell the land over and over."

"That is complicated. Not to mention sort of risky. Who the hell did they think was going to fall for that after the first time?" They both laughed, and Tabby answered her phone when it rang. Joey looked out the window as they drove toward the huge house on the outskirts of town.

"Change of plans. Elly is in labor, and Cain wants us all there." The car made a turn, then another, and they were headed in the opposite direction. "I'm to also tell you that Caleb called Windermere's boss. He'll have a nice long talk to the man when he meets us at the hospital. I don't know about you, but Windermere made it sound like he was in charge of the entire force. Whatever. We're going there to see the newest member of the family to arrive."

The hospital wasn't all that large, but it was well maintained. He loved the stained glassed windows that greeted a person when they walked in. Also, he noticed that there were large pots of plants all over the inside and out. As they were headed to the elevators, a large stained-glass mural from the top of the hall shone down on the floor to make the most beautiful scene he'd ever seen done in glass.

The two of them stopped at the shop just before they got into the elevator. He'd seen women shop before, of course. His mom was a pro at it. She'd have a cart full of food for the household and enough coupons to make it all be less than fifty bucks. His mom could make a dollar scream, his dad used to say, to make it worth more. Joey was never sure how that worked, but it was funny. Tabby could have made an art of it too. They were getting into the elevator when he finally spoke to her about her purchases.

"You do know that this kid isn't going to care if you got it a bow that was pink or yellow

when it's born, don't you?" She grinned at him.
"I'm also reasonably sure it won't give a shit
what sort of vase the pretty flowers are in that
you bought."

"I will care. Besides, Elly will love it too.
Caleb said she's pretty beat up. Did you see that
too?" He nodded but didn't elaborate. "I guess
you've seen all kinds of things at the end of your
weapon. I'm glad you didn't tell me. I don't
know that I could be any less hurt about her
being kidnapped. By her own father, no less."

"She's safe now. That's all you should
focus on." She thanked him. "Also, you might
want to take a minute to get yourself in a better
place. If you go in there crying, your husband is
going to knock me on my ass before I get to tell
him you're a sappy woman and that I didn't hurt
you."

It worked. She was laughing when the
doors opened, and Caleb was there waiting for
them. Taking the teddy bear from him, Caleb
shook his hand and thanked him once again.
Joey said he'd like to just move on with his life
now. Caleb told him that Windermere had been
taken care of.

"While I'm glad he's not going to hunt me

down, what exactly do you mean that he's been taken care of?" There was laugher behind Caleb, but he was more interested in the man in front of him. "Caleb, please tell me that you didn't kill that man. He's a prick, yes, but he was also a fed. And even though he was a royal pain in the ass, I'm sure someone is going to question what happened to him."

"I fired him." The man came out from behind Caleb and shook his hand as well. It took Joey a full thirty seconds to realize who he was shaking hands with. As soon as his hand was released, he saluted the president. "No need for that, Joey. The man was a tyrant. Not to mention, him telling you to shoot the woman and let Douglas live was against everything I believe in. Caleb said you were going to be working for him and his family."

"I am, sir." Joey glanced at Caleb before looking at the president. "You know Caleb? That's who he said he was going to call?"

"Yes, well, I knew his mother much better. Abby is the one that convinced me I needed to get my ass in gear and run this country. By saying she convinced me, I'm being very kind. She was a hellion when it suited her." Since he'd not known the other woman, he just nodded. "I only came by to make sure you knew that you aren't in any trouble with what you did here today. You saved a life. And perhaps, as you told Windermere, the future president of the United States."

When he left, surrounded by the men that were there to protect him, Joey hugged Caleb. "You're turning out to be the best brother a man could have; I hope you realize that." They were both laughing when they sat down. "I'm not kidding you; you know that, don't you?"

"I do. And you're wonderful as well. Now, let's discuss what sort of things you're going to need to make sure something like this never happens again. All right?"

Joey couldn't have been happier than he was at this very moment. He had a brother, a place to live, and a job. Food in his belly was a big thing as well. And tonight, he was going to help hand out blankets and hot meals in their own town. Joey thought he could live like this for the rest of his days and not need another thing.

~*~

Yasmine started to sit up, but the pain behind her eyes had her crying out. Stopping all movement other than to lie back on the pillow, she wondered not just where she was but what had happened to get her there.

The squeak of shoes told her she was in some sort of medical facility. She'd been in enough of those over her life that even the smell of antiseptic would make her blood run cold. Not that anyone at any facility had ever been mean to her. It was just being there over and over that had her cringe whenever she smelled certain smells.

"Yasmine Dennis?" Turning her head toward the voice, she said that was her name. "My name is Doctor Jerome. Do you know where you are?"

"Medical facility." He asked her which one. "I don't know. Has anyone notified my sister? Jasmine Dennis?"

"We've called her, but she's not arrived just yet. What can you tell me about what had you coming in here tonight?" Yasmine didn't know, but she had a feeling that not only did this man know, but he wasn't terribly happy about the turn of events that brought her here. "The police are here, Miss Dennis. They have a few questions for you about why you're here."

"All right. But I'd like to wait on my sister,

please?" Dr. Jerome told her they were only going to be a moment. "I'd rather you didn't bring them in. I want to wait on my sister. You said you called her, but she's not here. I want to wait on her."

"Miss Dennis? My name is Captain Sawyer. I'd like to ask you a few questions if you'd not mind." She told him she did mind, and she wanted her sister there. "Miss Dennis, you're not in trouble. We're just here to ask you some things about last night. Do you own a car, Miss Dennis?"

"No. I will keep telling you until she's here that I want to wait on my sister. It's important that she be here with me." He asked her two more questions, each of them sounding a little harsher like he was angry with her now. "I would like my sister, Jasmine Dennis, here before I answer any questions you put before me."

After about the fifth time she repeated her statement, they seemed to get the idea. They weren't happy about it, but they no longer peppered her with questions.

Hearing the door open, she knew it was going to be her sister.

"Yazzie?" Thank goodness. "My goodness,

what's happened to you? Why are the police here? Tell me what's going on."

"I don't know. I woke up in here, and they're asking me questions." Her sister asked someone what was going on. "Jasmine, just don't get arrested."

"We're just asking questions, for now, Miss Dennis. Some witnesses put your sister behind the wheel of a car that was the getaway vehicle for an armed robbery yesterday afternoon. There are seven dead plus three officers. We'd like to know where she was and who she was with."

"You're joking right now, aren't you?" Jasmine's fingers tightened around hers before her sister continued. "Well, I guess I can see where you'd not know. Gentlemen, I can tell you right now that there isn't any way the witness was telling you the truth. My sister has been blind since we were seven years old. There isn't any way she'd drive anything anywhere."

Jasmine made it sound like she'd won a marathon or something. That she'd come in first, too. Being blind wasn't anything Yasmine had wanted, but it had happened, and here she was. While the police asked questions of her sister, Yasmine tried to focus on anything but the fact that she was a little excited that someone, even for a brief time, thought she could be a regular person and drive a car.

"They're gone." Jasmine climbed into the bed with her and held her hands. "Your face is pretty beat up. There are bandages on your eyes. I told you to get one of those bracelet things that will tell people you're blind. What would you have done had I not come in here and saved your ass?"

"Gone to jail." Jasmine told her to be sensible. "I would have gotten around to it sooner or later, Jasmine. It's not like I would have been able to hide the fact that I can't see from them once they asked me to look at pictures or something. Just let me lie here in the quiet for a moment."

It had only been lately that Yasmine was getting annoyed with her twin. She was forever bossing her around about this or that. Usually, things that Yasmine didn't want to do, or for that matter, didn't think necessary. Like the shirt.

Jasmine had gotten her a new shirt. She brought it to her apartment and had her try it on. She wore it for most of the first afternoon. It wasn't until she was brought back to her place after being at the mall with her that Hal, her landlord, had told her what the shirt said. "I'm blind, so pardon me for stumbling around."

The thing was, Jasmine wouldn't have seen it as a joke. Getting her a shirt that pointed out her blindness and made a big deal out of it was something that Jasmine was really good about doing. No matter how much it embarrassed Yasmine, her sister thought the world should be aware that her twin was handicapped. A word that Jasmine loved as much as Yasmine hated.

"You'll come and stay with me for a few days." Yasmine didn't bother telling her no. She wouldn't be bullied into anything at this point in her life. "That way, I can pamper you and care for you."

"I don't need caring for, Jazzy. I'm fine." She told her that she'd been beaten. "Perhaps, but it's not like I can see any more than I did before the bandages were put on my face. I'm not going home with you. I don't like your menagerie of animals. Nor do I care for all the noises at your place. The sounds or the smells."

"My home does not smell. And you'll stay with me, and that's final." Though it wasn't nearly final, Yasmine didn't say anything to her.

"What is this world coming to when people are killed in a bank robbery?"

"You sound like you're rooting for the bank robbers." Yasmine was feeling sleepy and asked Jasmine to move off the bed. Of course, she had to put up a fuss. "Jasmine, blind or not, I was hurt. Just let me rest."

Calling for the nurse, her sister was just pissed off enough that she wouldn't speak to either of them. It wasn't like anyone looking at the two of them would think they were anything but related. The nurse winked at her when Jasmine didn't answer her question about the two of them being related. The only difference between the two of them that Yasmine was aware of was that her sister was annoying, and she wasn't. Laughing a little to herself, the door opened and closed before she felt the medicine kick in.

"Do you need anything else, honey?" Yasmine asked the nurse, who she assumed was giving her the medicine, where her sister had gone. "I think she's in a huff, that one. Upset because you called me in here, I guess. If you're hurting, honey, don't hesitate to call. Did they tell you how you're injured? Someone should have guessed that you couldn't see. Let me go get your chart and tell you." The door opened briefly then closed up. "Let me see here."

"You knew I was blind." The nurse, Anna, told her she had been in the room when she'd awakened. "I don't understand. I mean, I'm glad you figured it out, but how?"

"You didn't look around." She laughed a little. "It says here that you have a concussion, as well as a sprained ankle. There are fifteen stitches in your forehead, as well as numerous lacerations to your face and neck. Nothing is broken. Is there anything else I can help you with, honey?"

"No." She thought about it. "Yes. Wait. I know this is going to sound very odd, but I was wondering if you could call a friend of mine. I know his number. His name is Caleb Anderson. But I don't want you to tell my sister. She'll get all up in my face about calling someone else to help me out."

"I can do that for you." The phone was picked up, and she heard the buttons pressed. "If you don't mind my saying so, child, I think you should try and distance yourself from your sister for a bit. She's trying very hard to control you. Yes. My name is Anna Dereck. I'm a nurse at Mercy Hospital. I have a patient of mine that would like to speak with Mr. Caleb Anderson."

Control her? Yes, she supposed it would look like Jasmine was trying to control her when all she was doing was trying to keep her safe. Sometimes she did take things too far, and there were times, like now, that she wanted to get away from her. But controlling her?

The phone was put into her hand, and she said her name.

"Hello, Yasmine Dennis. My name is Tabby Anderson. I'm Caleb's wife. He's not here right now, but I can get a message to him if you'd like." Yasmine told the other woman it was all right. It wasn't important. "I think it is. You're obviously in a hospital. Emergency room? No. It's too quiet there. What is it I can tell Caleb so he can fix whatever is wrong?"

"It's nothing, Mrs. Anderson." She said her name was Tabby. "Yes, I understand. We're friends, Caleb and me. Or we were sort of friends. I'm not sure we still are. It's been a long time, so he might not remember me at all. Well, I don't know how many blind women he knows, but I'm sure that would be the only stand out that would jar his memory."

"Are you finished ranting?" Yasmine told her she didn't feel she was ranting. "All right. Then are you finished over explaining why you'd be calling a married man? I'm assuming that's why you're rambling. I guess that would be a better word for it."

"I've been hurt, you see. I'm in the hospital with a concussion. A sprained ankle too, but since I've not gotten up, I don't know if it hurts or not. The nurse who called for me just gave me some medication for pain, so that might be it." She felt secure in talking to this woman because she knew the chances of meeting her were slim to none. "My sister, my twin, is driving me crazy. She's… well, I was just told she's controlling. I didn't realize that before. Or maybe I did, and that was why I called you. Or Caleb. Understand?"

"I do. And even though you know you're hurt and could use someone to help you along, you don't want it to be her. Is that right?" Yasmine said that was it precisely. "You're at Mercy, the nurse said."

"Yes. But please don't bother Caleb. I was just having a moment, and now that I'm over it, I'm all right to go home with Jasmine." Before she could stop herself, Yasmine spoke again. "She has four cats and two dogs. Last time I was at her house, she had a ferret and a bird. It's very noisy at her house too. Like animals baying at the moon kind of noises." The laughter alerted her that she'd spoken aloud. "I'm sorry. You must think I'm an ungrateful sister that needs to be slapped."

"I don't, actually. I find you totally honest and fun." The door opened and closed, and she knew it was her sister by her smell. "I guess you have company now. I'll see you later, Yasmine."

"Who was that?" She told her it was a friend of hers from college. "A better friend than I am a sister? Never mind. Don't answer that. I'm sorry I got in a huff about you staying with me. But I do think it's the only way to go. You'll come and stay with me, and we'll have some fun for a while. I'll get on your nerves, and you'll go home, and we'll have a few days to reflect on how much we annoy each other before we're calling again. All right?"

Yasmine was saved from answering when her phone rang. Of course, her sister answered it and didn't even bother handing the phone to her, but just started talking to the person on the other end.

"She's asleep." Whoever it was laughed, and Yasmine had a feeling it was Tabby Anderson. "When I tell you she's asleep, then she's asleep. Who is this?"

"Give me the phone, Jasmine. I want to talk to her." Of course, she didn't. Nor did she stop telling the woman she was asleep when she had to be able to hear her talking to her sister. Then the phone slammed down on the cradle. "Why did you do that? I told you I wanted to talk to her. Jasmine, that was just rude."

"That woman was rude. She said to tell you she had your ass. What the hell is that supposed to mean? Then she laughed at me. Like it was some kind of joke that I was trying to let you rest, as you told me you wanted to do." She did want her to let her rest, but as usual, Jasmine wouldn't do what she wanted. However, it wasn't worth fighting with her about what she wanted. "I'm going to talk to the staff and tell them you're not to have any visitors. It would be just like that rude woman to come here and try to take you from me."

"I'm not a child, Jasmine. There isn't any way she's going to kidnap me." Jasmine told her it wouldn't happen while she was there. "You're being ridiculous. Next time she calls, you hand me the phone."

"I will not. It's settled. I don't know how you think you're going to get along at home without someone there to take care of you, Yasmine. I told you it was settled, and it is. I'm responsible for you, and I take that very seriously." Jasmine had said that to her before. A lot. "Now, tell me what she said and who her name is so I can take care of this for you."

"Linda Ashcraft. She and I went to school together." Jasmine left her then, the door opening and closing told her that. Plus, she could no longer smell the cats on her sister's clothing. Yasmine smiled. "She's not going to be bothered by not coming to see me because she died some time ago. Good luck, Tabby, if you're coming here. It's going to be a nightmare for us both, I think."

Before You Go...

HELP AN AUTHOR

write a review

THANK YOU!

Share your voice and help guide other readers to these wonderful books. Even if it's only a line or two, your reviews help readers discover the author's books so they can continue creating stories that you'll love. Log in to your favorite retailer and leave a review. Thank you.

AWARD WINNING, BESTSELLING AUTHOR

Kathi Barton, a winner of the Pinnacle Book Achievement award as well as a best-selling author on Amazon and All Romance books, lives in Nashport, Ohio, with her husband, Paul. When not creating new worlds and romance, Kathi and her husband enjoy camping and going to auctions. She can also be seen at county fairs with her husband, who is an artist and potter.

Her muse, a cross between Jimmy Stewart and Hugh Jackman, brings her stories to life for her readers in a way that has them coming back time and again for more. Her favorite genre is paranormal romance, with a great deal of spice. You can visit Kathi online and drop her an email if you'd like. She loves hearing from her fans. aaronskiss@gmail.com.

Follow Kathi on her blog: http://kathisbartonauthor.blogspot.com/